MONTANA MAVERICKS

Welcome to Big Sky Country, home of the Montana Mavericks! Where free-spirited men and women discover love on the range.

THE TRAIL TO TENACITY

Tenacity is the town that time forgot, home of down-to-earth cowboys who'd give you the (denim) shirt off their back. Through the toughest times, they've held their heads high, and they've never lost hope. Take a ride out this way and get to know the neighbors—you might even meet the maverick of your dreams!

With her biological clock ticking, Allison Taylor knows she should be trying harder to find someone, but all her dates pale in comparison to her handsome neighbor Rowan Scott. They've been "just friends" for so long, and their timing has always been off. She knows asking him to be her fake date for the holidays is bananas. Or could it be the start of something big?

Dear Reader,

I hope you love Christmas as much as I do!

I wrote much of this book during the holidays last year. Some authors have to re-create Christmas during the summer they are writing their book, and honestly, that's not a bad idea. I was lucky enough to have Christmas going on all around me as I was writing. The tree was up in mid-November, and I happily posted a photo on social media with the words: *No, it's not too soon*.

For me, the holidays are a time for decorating with wreaths and garlands, baking, family get-togethers, big dinners, tree lighting ceremonies, parades and cookie exchanges. (Did somebody say *cookie*? No wonder I love this holiday!) These activities are some of the fun our heroine, Allison Taylor, and her friend Rowan Scott get into this season. They are forced to fake being in love, and what do you know, it happens for real. That's Christmas for you. Love is the biggest gift of all.

From my house to yours, I wish you a joyous and safe holiday season.

Happy reading—and happy holidays!

Heatherly Bell

THE MAVERICK'S CHRISTMAS COUNTDOWN

HEATHERLY BELL

MONTANA MAVERICKS

Special thanks and acknowledgment are given to Heatherly Bell for her contribution to the Montana Mavericks: The Trail to Tenacity miniseries.

Harlequin®
MONTANA MAVERICKS

Recycling programs for this product may not exist in your area.

ISBN-13: 978-1-335-14316-7

The Maverick's Christmas Countdown

Copyright © 2024 by Harlequin Enterprises ULC

Harlequin Enterprises ULC
22 Adelaide St. West, 41st Floor
Toronto, Ontario M5H 4E3, Canada
www.Harlequin.com

Printed in Lithuania

MIX
Paper | Supporting responsible forestry
FSC® C021394

Bestselling author **Heatherly Bell** was born in Tuscaloosa, Alabama, but lost her accent by the time she was two. After leaving Alabama, Heatherly lived with her family in Puerto Rico and Maryland before being transplanted kicking and screaming to the California Bay Area. She now loves it here, she swears. Except the traffic.

Books by Heatherly Bell

Montana Mavericks: The Trail to Tenacity

The Maverick's Christmas Countdown

Harlequin Special Edition

Charming, Texas

Winning Mr. Charming
The Charming Checklist
A Charming Christmas Arrangement
A Charming Single Dad
A Charming Doorstep Baby
Once Upon a Charming Bookshop
Her Fake Boyfriend

The Fortunes of Texas: Hitting the Jackpot

Winning Her Fortune

Montana Mavericks: The Real Cowboys of Bronco Heights

Grand-Prize Cowboy

Wildfire Ridge

More than One Night
Reluctant Hometown Hero
The Right Moment

Visit the Author Profile page
at Harlequin.com for more titles.

To everyone who loves Christmas.

Chapter One

"English was my favorite subject in high school," Allison Taylor said from her stool at the kitchen counter.

On this sunny December day in Bronco, she was helping her niece, Jill Abernathy, with her homework.

"I'm more of a math and science person, and I don't know what to do with this assignment." Jill's big eyes were narrowed in confusion. "I'm supposed to pick a book and then find a parallel to something in my own life."

Allison rubbed her hands together. "Oooh, it sounds like an essay, my favorite kind of assignment!"

"I wish it were *already* Christmas break. Then I could have some fun and relax." Jill's shoulders slumped. "Would you help me figure this out? I don't know how a book is anything like real life!"

Allison had been about Jill's age when her older sister Charlotte and Billy Abernathy had first fallen in love as teenagers. His daughter was now Charlotte's stepdaughter, and reminded Allison so much of her father as a teen. Same eyes, same easygoing attitude. But, at the moment, she was clearly frustrated, as though there was so much she'd rather do than sit inside with a book. Just like Billy, who'd always preferred to spend his time running the Bonnie B ranch. According to Charlotte, Jill had demonstrated an aptitude in math and science, but she was still finding her way as a fourteen-year-old in her first year of high school. Allison would let her sister encourage all things STEM, but she would do what she could to encourage a love of reading.

"Actually your life is probably a lot more like a Western book." Allison chuckled.

"Ugh, I'm sick of cowboys. Bronco's just a boring town full of cowboys."

"How about a Christmas theme? Then you can tie it into what you're doing right now. Looking forward to the holiday. Shopping, decorating, gift giving." Allison couldn't help but make at least one specific suggestion. "One of *my* favorite holiday stories is *The Gift of the Magi*. It's a classic. You should check it out."

"Great idea. Thanks, Aunt Allison!" Jill stood and rushed up the steps, past Charlotte, who was slowly coming down them.

Charlotte padded into the kitchen in her robe and slippers, fresh from a nap. She was due soon, a scheduled C-section next month. At thirty-eight, she'd been ordered to take it easy for the rest of the pregnancy.

"You're so good with her. The boys, too. Face it, you're good with kids."

Allison sighed. She didn't want to dwell on the envy she felt rolling through her every time she looked at Charlotte's swollen belly or felt the baby's swift kick against her palm. Her big sister deserved all this joy and happiness and more. Over twenty years ago, she'd been a pregnant teenager with Billy's child, but had had a devastating miscarriage a few weeks into the pregnancy. Even though they were still to get married, in a rather huge wedding thrown by the Taylors and Abernathys, seventeen-year-old Charlotte had had second thoughts. She'd abandoned Billy at the altar to fulfill her dream of becoming a marine biologist.

She and Billy had spent over two decades apart but were together now, and it was a beautiful thing to watch.

Allison stood to pour hot water from the kettle into a mug. "Maybe it's because your stepkids are great. Anyway, someday I'll meet the right man."

"Whatever happened to that guy you were dating a few months ago? He sounded so promising."

"Don't remind me. He was a dud dressed in prince clothing."

Allison still cringed remembering the way he'd invited her to a fancy dinner just to inform her he worried she was getting way too attached to their relationship.

"I think we might want different things," he'd said in a patronizing tone that had made her want to down her pricy cocktail as fast as possible. "I'm not ready to settle down, and I can see the eagerness in your eyes. After all, I'm only thirty-eight."

For the record, there had been no such eagerness on her part.

Charlotte made a face. "I'm sorry. You've sure had to kiss a lot of frogs."

"Look at it this way, thanks partly to him, you now have a built-in babysitter."

"Except when you're back in Seattle."

"Well, I'm here at least until the baby is born."

Fortunately, Allison had enough vacation time accrued from her job as a human resource specialist to take a month off to be with her older sister and help her family.

"I'm glad you're here." Charlotte accepted the mug of hot water and dipped her herbal cinnamon tea bag inside. "But you may have overstepped at Thanksgiving. What are you going to do if Mom and Dad ask to *meet* this fake boyfriend of yours? You've already had him out of the country once."

Charlotte had asked the question of the year.

Allison would rather not dwell on this unfortunate complication and simply enjoy all the holiday festivities with her sister's blended family. She wanted to relax and enjoy the most magical time of the year, but Charlotte was correct. She had a teeny problem.

At Thanksgiving dinner with her family last month, she'd lied about having a serious boyfriend. In her defense, her parents had been openly trying to fix her up with Frederick Lloyd Huntington III, one of her father Thaddeus Taylor's oldest friends and business partners. A man even richer than her father—and at least twenty years her senior.

"It's time you settled down, young lady," her father Thaddeus had pronounced just after the turkey had been carved and served. "Frederick is a fine man. He's expressed interest and I've decided he's worthy."

"That biological clock is ticking!" Imogen, her mother, had shaken a finger. "You don't want to wait too long. Look at Charlotte."

Zero preliminaries. Straight from slicing turkey to slicing into Allison. She hardly needed the memo about her biological clock. It ticked in her ear like a time bomb most days.

"You can all stop worrying about me. I won't be able to marry Frederick since I'm dating someone new and it's very serious."

"Can he support himself?" Thaddeus had snorted. "Or is he an *artist?*"

"He is, in fact, a *doctor.* So, yes, he can, in fact, support himself, and quite nicely. The only reason he's not here with me is because he had a previous commitment to Doctors Without Borders."

Her sisters Eloise and Charlotte had glanced up in surprise. They'd known she hadn't been dating anyone since the software engineer who hadn't worked out. No one had worked out. And, frankly, she was happy enough single. She had friends in Seattle and work that satisfied her. The problem was, in the quiet of the night she had to admit the truth to herself, even if to no one else: she wanted to have children. And she was old-fashioned enough to want it all. Marriage to a wonderful man like the ones her sisters had been lucky enough to find.

"Wonderful!" Imogen had said after a gasp of surprise. "I'm so happy to hear this."

"Doctors make lousy husbands," Thaddeus had muttered. "They're never home."

She'd apparently never make her *father* happy, so Allison had long ago stopped trying. The lie had come swiftly and effortlessly because she'd been so tired of hearing about Frederick. Her father thought he could rule her life, which was why she didn't come home to Montana often. But Charlotte needed her, and she was one person Allison would never disappoint.

"I'll think of some excuse why the doctor can't be here," Allison said now, putting away a clean dish left lying on the counter by one of the kids. "In all fairness, when I lied about my boyfriend—"

"The *doctor*," Charlotte interrupted.

"Right. The doctor. I didn't know I'd be staying with you for the holidays."

"Hey, don't blame me. This is what happens when you have a 'geriatric' pregnancy." Charlotte held up air quotes.

"Now I have to stay off my feet as much as possible for the rest of the pregnancy."

"It wasn't a problem. I usually come out for a few days every Christmas anyway."

"But this is much longer than you're used to dealing with Thaddeus, and I appreciate you being here. I know it isn't easy."

Charlotte reached across the counter to pat Allison's hand. She'd had her own struggles with their father.

"Anything for you, sis."

Truthfully, she would have preferred spending the holidays in her adopted city of Seattle among her good friends and neighbors. But when Charlotte had asked Allison to come and stay a little longer this time, to get her through the end of a difficult pregnancy, Allison hadn't been able to turn her down.

She might not be able to stand her ruthless father, but her mother was okay. And Allison adored Charlotte, Billy and their family. Now there would be another little one coming along soon. Charlotte and Billy's only child. Their five-bedroom farmhouse would soon be busting at the seams. Allison was staying in the nursery now, and every morning she woke to a beautiful mural of dolphins and sea life perfect for the daughter of a marine biologist. Charlotte was on maternity leave from her position at Wonderstone Ridge Indoor Theme Park and Aquarium. Because Charlotte had had an amniocentesis, she'd decided to find out the sex of her child. A little girl, though she hadn't told Billy, who wanted to be surprised. And if Allison knew her sister, the act of keeping such monumental news a secret may have been compromised at some point. So far, Billy seemed clueless so the surprise hadn't been ruined for him.

Just the idea of a baby girl in the Abernathy household

and the sister that Jill would now have thrilled Allison to bits, and all the excitement surrounding the new Abernathy baby had infected her.

"See if this imaginary boyfriend of yours can get you pregnant." Charlotte echoed Allison's thoughts. "If you're not careful, you'll be like me. A geriatric mother."

Allison made a face. "You're not a geriatric *mother*, you have a geriatric pregnancy."

"Potato, potahto," Charlotte said. "I feel so old when I hear the word *geriatric* in reference to me."

"Anyway, I don't care if I wind up like you. I *want* to be like you. Look at you, you're doing great. The most important thing is to have a partner who supports you all the way, and you have that. You couldn't do better than Billy."

"So true," Charlotte sighed, no doubt thinking of her handsome rancher husband. "He was worth waiting for. But you're going to be a great mother. My stepkids already love you probably more than they love me."

"I doubt that."

Allison was enjoying spending time with Billy's children by his first marriage, Nicky and Jill. The oldest, Branson, was away at college for the first time, getting ready to come home for holiday break after finishing his first semester at the University of Montana. He'd wanted to skip higher education and simply be a rancher like his father and hadn't seen the point of an education. Thankfully, his parents had felt differently. All three of Charlotte's stepchildren were amazing, but Allison was a little partial to Jill. She was always so clear in her thoughts, holding nothing back. If she was having a bad day, everybody knew it. And with a father like Billy, she obviously felt comfortable expressing her feelings.

Unlike Jill, growing up, Allison had never had an easy

time expressing herself in a household where Thaddeus had taken away anything she'd ever cared about. She'd been shipped off to boarding school over her protests. Her punishment because her *sister* had gotten pregnant before marriage and one evening Thaddeus had overheard Allison talking about the cute new boy at school. "Best to nip that in the bud," he'd ordered. No more unmarried and pregnant daughters! When Allison had heard about their youngest sister Eloise's out-of-wedlock pregnancy, even if years later, Allison had had a good laugh.

Because of all this, she'd learned to keep her desires and private thoughts to herself. She hadn't expected the tendency to spill over into all areas of her life, but now found it second nature to be protective and secretive when she truly wanted something. She was suspicious, as if she might "jinx" something by saying the words out loud.

Even now, Allison had trouble expressing to her own sister how much she wanted a baby of her own. Someday, maybe. If it happened to her sister, it could happen to Allison, who was two years younger. But she better get on that.

"You could always adopt, if it comes to that." Charlotte stirred organic milk into her tea. "Did you hear about Baby J? He was found at the church, wrapped up in blankets, in a Moses basket. Can you imagine?"

"Have they had any luck finding the mother?"

"Not so far. His mother must have been desperate to abandon her baby, especially like that."

Allison agreed. "I hope they're reunited, and soon."

Charlotte brightened. "Hey, maybe you could adopt him! Would you ever consider adoption?"

Allison would love to adopt, but she could already see the scowl of disapproval on Thaddeus's face. If she so much as mentioned any interest, too, he'd probably find a way to intervene and make sure it didn't happen.

"Can you imagine how our parents would react to my adopting a baby without knowing anything about his background?"

Charlotte sighed. "You're right. Not that I think it matters, you understand. Hopefully, Baby J will be reunited with his mother."

"That would be the ideal situation."

Allison was still thinking about the poor baby who'd been abandoned by his mother when her phone rang with a video call.

She glanced to see the caller. "I have to take this."

Charlotte stretched her arms and yawned. "Go ahead. I think I'll go lie down. If I fall asleep, wake me when Billy gets here?"

"I would, but he's the one always running upstairs to wake you." Allison hustled up the steps to the nursery to answer her phone.

The video call displayed Rowan Scott, her friend and neighbor at her apartment complex in Seattle. She'd asked him to water her plants and bring in the mail while she was gone.

"Hey," Allison said. "Everything okay? Please don't tell me I've had a flood or some other disaster."

"Nothing like that." Rowan turned the screen to show a lineup of her three ferns sitting side by side. "Just checking in. Larry, Mo and Curly are doing fine, as you can see. And, yeah, I've named your plants. Hey, also don't forget that I'm hosting casino night in your apartment every night. Going well so far. I'll deal you in on the action, not to worry. We're going to make some serious coin. Sixty/forty, right? It's your apartment, but I'm doing all the work."

"Ha, ha. You better not be having fun like that without me."

She and Rowan had been buddies since the day she'd moved in across the hallway from his apartment and he'd helped carry the heaviest of her boxes. He was just that kind of a guy; always helpful, always seeming to have a smile on his face when she saw him.

"Sorry, I have to joke to mask my true feelings." He turned the image back on himself and for the first time she noticed the tightness in his mouth, the bags under his eyes.

Rowan was forever cracking jokes and rarely serious. She couldn't imagine why he'd be sad.

"What's wrong?"

He worked as a data analyst for a major software firm, a well-paying tech job he did from home and could do from almost anywhere. This made him convenient for plant watering and mail gathering, and she certainly hoped he hadn't been laid off. Not right before the holidays. As the director of human resources at another software giant, she'd told her HR colleagues before she'd left for her vacation, "Tell all managers: absolutely no layoffs while I'm gone. It's Christmas!"

"Perri. We broke up again. And without you here to help me drown my sorrows in Pinot Grigio, I've had to resort to Three Stooges' and casino night jokes."

"Oh, I'm sorry. Not again. Who broke things off this time?"

Rowan and his girlfriend broke up every few months and, by Allison's calculations, this was right on schedule. If it wasn't her breaking up with him, it was Rowan breaking up with Perri, tired of her drama. Then one or the other would decide to give it another try and the madness would start all over again. It was getting to where Allison could practically set a clock by their breakups.

"She broke up with me this time. Via text message. Classy, right?"

Allison groaned. "That's a new low."

"This is it. I can't keep doing this to myself. I'm moving on. Perri and I are not right for each other. I've known it for a while."

So had Allison, and all of their mutual friends, but even now she refused to say anything. He'd said those very same words to her in the past. She couldn't trust those two wouldn't get back together again, especially during the holidays when nostalgia deepened. Take it from her, being single at Christmas was not an ideal situation. She ached for Rowan as the timing couldn't be much worse.

"What was her reasoning?"

"I'm not *serious* enough for her."

"What? You're a jokester. Fun. That's your personality."

"Yeah, well, obviously she doesn't like my personality." He shrugged.

"That's ridiculous. You've got a great personality."

Allison's mind briefly went to those old lame fix-up jokes. "Let me fix you two up. He's got a *great* personality." This usually implied looks weren't optimal, which certainly didn't apply to Rowan. He actually didn't *need* a personality with looks like his, but God had thrown it in anyway. Rowan was classic matinee-idol handsome with dark wavy hair, blue eyes and a jaw that could cut glass. His looks and good character were wasted on Perri. Though the woman was beautiful, she had zero personality.

"So, who are you spending the holidays with?"

Rowan held up one of Allison's plants and winked. "Nothing until Christmas Day with the fam at my brother's. For now, I'm hanging with my new best friend here and cleaning up at casino night."

Allison didn't like the idea of Rowan alone until Christmas. If he were here, she could keep him busy and take his thoughts off Perri. It was what she'd do if she were back home in Seattle. Take him out for a drink, let him unload.

Now that she'd thought of it, having him come to Bronco might not be a bad thing. There was always so much going on in a full household like the Abernathys that even Allison didn't have time to dwell on her troubles. The fact that she was still single and now faking a relationship was something she could ignore for entire stretches of time between laundry and picking up kids from school. If she were to put him in charge of some of these tasks, he'd soon be too busy to be upset about his breakup.

Allison tipped her head. "Hmm. I have an idea. Can you get Mrs. Havisham in 2C to water my plants?"

Her name wasn't actually Mrs. Havisham but Allison and Rowan nicknamed her after the Dickens character for fun. Twice, she'd answered her door with only one shoe on, so she'd "walked" right into that one.

"Why?" He glanced sideways at her ferns, still mercifully alive. "Does one of them look sick? I thought green was the only requirement."

"No, silly! I can't stand you being alone and feeling sad, and I want you to come to Montana. Spend some time here with me and my family. We'd love to have you."

"Are you serious?"

"There's plenty of room at my sister's place and I could use the help. I'm doing all the cooking, cleaning, decorating and shuttling around of two teenagers."

"What a nice offer. I look forward to you turning me into Cinderella for the holidays."

"I promise you'll have fun. We have so many small-town holiday festivities around here. Have you ever had a down-home Christmas, Montana-style?" Allison happened to know Rowan was born and bred in Washington state.

"You *know* I haven't."

"Then I say it's time."

In fact, he'd never visited Allison's hometown even if she talked about it frequently enough. No one had ever met him. Wait.

No one in her family had ever *met* Rowan.

Perfect.

This idea was so crazy that it might actually work.

"I take it back. You don't have to help me with any of the cooking and cleaning. What if you help me in another far more important way? In return, I have one favor to ask of you."

"What's that?"

"Pretend to be my boyfriend while you're here?" She winced. "I'm in trouble. Remember when I lied to my parents at Thanksgiving, said I was dating someone, and it was serious? Well, now that I'm here for a month, they're bound to press me about my boyfriend. You know, the one that doesn't exist? And if I tell them some other lie about how he can't be here, *again*, they're definitely never going to believe he exists."

"Well, so what? He *doesn't* exist. You don't have a boyfriend. It's not the end of the world."

"Um, remember Frederick III? He's conveniently still single. Shocker. And if I'm here, all alone, they're going to hoist him on me. They won't stop. It won't work, of course, which will only make the holidays awkward and difficult to get through. I wanted them to give up trying."

"I knew you'd get yourself into trouble by lying. But... didn't you tell them your boyfriend is a doctor?"

"Um, yes. That's right. It sounded impressive. My father made some snarky remark about a starving artist, and it was the perfect comeback."

"Not so perfect. I can't pretend to be a doctor! I can't even spell Naproxen."

"You can fake it."

"Oh sure. I'll see if I can sign up for an online course somewhere. 'How to be a doctor in thirty minutes or less.'"

"You're a data analyst. Do an analysis of doctor personalities and assume one of those identities."

"That's...not how this works." He shook his head and fought a smile.

"Pretty please?" Allison batted her eyelashes. "I miss you. It will be like having a little piece of Seattle with me through the holidays. Best of both worlds for me."

"All right, *fine*. I'll come for a few days, but you owe me for this. *Big* time. In fact, you might have to put me in your will."

"Thank you, thank you!" Allison said. "I can't wait."

When her parents, especially her *mother*, got one look at Rowan, they'd know in an instant that Frederick III didn't stand a chance.

Faking would be easy for her, too, since she already had a wee but harmless crush on Rowan. She would never truly pursue him. Given his history with Perri, it was highly likely the two would be back together before Christmas. He'd go back home to Perri, having done his duty as her fake boyfriend and no one would ever be the wiser.

Chapter Two

Using the business airline miles he'd accumulated over the years of traveling, Rowan was able to score a ticket to Montana the next day.

"Toto, we're not in Kansas anymore," he muttered as he buckled up in the rideshare he'd ordered.

From the airport, the driver took him to a winter fairy-land, Western-style. They passed through the main street covered with festive green garlands hanging from every post and fence. A sign near a park proclaimed Christmas Tree Lighting Here Tonight. The tree was a mammoth pine that wouldn't look out of place in the forest.

"Yeah, we go all out here in Bronco," the driver said, waving an arm in one direction. "This is downtown. The tree lighting tonight is at the park between Bronco Heights and Bronco Valley, the two sides of town. We've got plenty of holiday shopping and also touristy stuff. Bronco Ghost Tours is in Bronco Heights, and it's always really popular at Halloween."

Rowan laughed, not realizing he would get a personal guided tour. "Bronco has *ghosts*?"

"Depends on who you believe. Run by Evan Cruise, and there's a history of psychics in his family, so, yeah, I think he believes."

"I'm visiting a good friend, so I'm sure she'll show me around."

Rowan spotted a store with some Western gear in the display window. He would get a pair of boots soon so he his entire look didn't scream "big city tourist."

Rowan was flattered when Allison said she'd missed him. She'd only asked him here to get out of a jam with her parents, but he would enjoy himself and her company. He refused to think of anything other than friendship between them as Allison had never expressed any interest, even during the times he and Perri were broken up. After this latest breakup, he thought he'd be more disappointed. It was Perri who'd talked him into giving them another chance two months ago and he'd caved.

Now, he'd come to a startling revelation. He'd always believed he didn't have much luck with relationships. But the truth was he always seemed to choose the wrong woman. He excelled at decisions elsewhere in his life, but when it came to romance, he made the wrong choice time and again. Whether it was his college girlfriend or any of the women he'd dated since then, it was almost as if he believed he couldn't do any better. He now doubted himself when it came to these decisions. His job for the next few months was to reevaluate everything. He'd stay single and figure out why he was continually drawn to women who felt that a relationship would complete their lives. Or who wanted him as an accessory, rather than a true partner. He tried but failed to find emotional satisfaction in those relationships.

No, he longed for a relationship with a woman who was fully independent. Someone who wanted a partner, but didn't need a man to feel complete. Someone like...

Allison.

This trip would be the distraction he needed and it was

the only reason he'd accepted Allison's invitation. This time, he was a little surprised by Perri's timing. During the holidays, she'd always loved their romantic celebrations—and it never hurt when he'd tried to go overboard with an expensive gift or two. He always delivered, because he'd also liked their holidays together. This year, though, something was different. After two years of dating on and off, he suspected she might think it was time for a ring, but he couldn't bring himself to get there.

Maybe Perri had sensed a ring wouldn't be forthcoming this Christmas and broken it off before he could disappoint her.

As he glanced out the window, he realized he was curious about the town where Allison had grown up. She'd told him a lot about this place, sometimes over happy hour cocktails with friends, or at a neighborhood Super Bowl party here and there over the time he'd known her. Once, they'd even double dated with whatever guy she'd been seeing at the time.

Rowan had noticed her memories of the town were equally intermixed with happiness and frustration. He understood it went all the way back to her father, Thaddeus Taylor, a wealthy rancher who tried to control every aspect of his six children's lives. Especially his three daughters. But that was a common enough occurrence among fathers of daughters, and he figured she'd exaggerated the situation.

Curiosity had driven him to look up the man's financial status. Thaddeus Taylor's Triple T ranch was quite a successful venture, and the man was co-owner, along with his brothers, of Taylor Beef, which supplied beef to all of the west and even farther. The man was worth millions. Rowan couldn't help but be shocked. Allison herself was so down to earth and likeable. He'd never seen her splurge on the latest fashions, shoes and bags the way Perri had. Allison could be found most of the time in a sweater and jeans, her chestnut-brown hair often up in a casual ponytail. It was her smile that drew most people in. Him, too, were he being honest. Her smile leaned a little toward the wicked, as did her laugh.

When he'd first met Allison, he was certain she had a husband or fiancé. No way would she be single with those looks and her friendly personality. And then later that day, not surprisingly, the boyfriend showed up to help. Rowan had made himself scarce, but that same night Allison knocked on his door to deliver a six-pack of beer as her thanks for his help.

Over the next few days, Rowan made jokes every time he'd run into her in the hallway, issuing himself a personal challenge to give her at least one belly laugh a day. By the time he realized she was once again free and single a few weeks after moving in, he'd already cemented his relationship with her as friend and neighbor. Friend-zoned.

Growing up with an older brother whose good looks were often compared to Henry Cavill's, Rowan had learned to rely on his personality. If he stood next to his brother, he became invisible. When he spinned his jokes, at least women would then notice and gravitate to him. He made a lot of friends that way, but been shocked when someone as outwardly gorgeous as Perri expressed her interest and gone after *him* for a change. And she'd come after him hard. It was flattering. Perri told him he was actually better looking than his brother and, much as he hated to admit it, she'd hit a tender spot with that compliment.

The driver had taken him miles out of town, into ranch country, and now they passed under a sign that announced the Bonnie B ranch. Some minutes later, he pulled over in front of a two-story farmhouse.

"This is it. The Bonnie B ranch."

It looked like something out of a movie. The exterior of the main house, covered in gray stone and brick, had a wraparound covered porch. The view of shady, leafy trees surrounding the house, rolling hills, and cattle grazing in the distance gave way to images of the old time Westerns he'd watched with his father as a kid. He had officially arrived in cattle country.

Rowan tipped the man, grabbed his bags and then slowly made his way up the stone-paved walkway. He took a moment to breathe in a whiff of fresh air. What people said was true. The oxygen had a better quality in the countryside.

Suddenly the front door flew open and Allison came rushing outside.

"You're here!"

"Hello, ma'am. I heard you're looking for extras for a Hallmark movie. All I need is a hot meal and I'll stand around wherever you need me."

"You would make a handsome cowboy and you can stand anywhere you like." She laughed and threaded her arm through his as they walked together up a slight incline toward the home.

"This place is amazing," he said, surveying the acreage surrounding them.

"This is all Abernathy land, and the entire family lives on some part of this huge property. My brother-in-law is devoted to the Bonnie B."

"A real cowboy, huh?"

"You could say that. Come inside and meet everyone. We've been waiting for you."

She went ahead of him and swung open a dark wood door layered with textured glass inserts.

"Rowan is here!"

She said this with the same enthusiasm a child might say Santa Claus had arrived. He followed her down the hall to a living room with gleaming wood floors, a wide leather sofa and several oversize chairs. A huge flat-screen dominated one wall, and another wall displayed a magnificent floor-to-ceiling fireplace.

A hugely pregnant woman with a passing resemblance to Allison waved to him from the couch. "Hello, Rowan. It's nice to finally meet you."

He set down his suitcase and walked toward her, bending to offer his hand. "You must be Charlotte. I've heard a lot about you."

"Same." She reached up to hug him instead. "Oh my goodness, you smell so *good*!"

Both Allison and the kids in the room burst out laughing.

Rowan bit on his lower lip to keep from making a joke.

"Take it easy, there." A tall, broad-shouldered man wearing a tan Stetson chuckled from nearby. "Don't forget you're married. I'm Billy Abernathy, Charlotte's husband."

He offered his hand and Rowan shook it. "Good to meet you."

"You always smell good, babe," Charlotte said, patting a space beside her on the couch. "Come sit with me."

"This is Nicky, Billy's son." Allison tapped the shoulder of a teenaged boy who looked a lot like his father. "And Jill, Billy's daughter."

Both kids respectfully shook his hand.

"You have a full house," Rowan said, tipping back on his heels.

"Our son Branson is away at university until winter

break, or it would be even fuller," Billy said. "You're right, with a baby on the way, we're busting at the seams."

"You'll take Branson's room until he gets back," Allison said. "Let me get you settled."

"Nice to meet you all. Thanks so much for inviting me for the holidays." Rowan waved and followed Allison up the staircase to a second-floor landing with a cathedral ceiling that gave a nice view of the cozy room below.

Rowan had checked the forecast and temps had dipped into the midthirties today, so he wasn't surprised to see Billy starting a fire in the hearth. Honestly, were the home not infused with touches of family photos and cozy knickknacks everywhere, he'd feel like a visitor at a rustic B and B in the countryside.

He dropped his suitcase inside a room that belonged to a teenage boy who clearly loved ranch life. There were 4-H ribbons hanging all over one wall, along with photos of horses and cattle. Otherwise, the room was spotless, meaning he hadn't been living there for a while.

Jill waved her hand toward the trophies. "Needless to say, Branson wants to be a rancher just like his dad."

"Obviously."

"But he got sent off to college anyway. I talked to him the other night when he called, and he can't wait to come home for an entire month."

"And the other kids? Do they also want to be ranchers like their father?"

"The gene may have bypassed them, but the Bonnie B will always be part of their lives in one way or another. Still, I doubt Billy will force any of his kids to take on ranching life. He's made it okay for them to follow their own path. Nicky loves music and he plays drums in the marching band. And Jill is still finding her way, though she and Charlotte bonded over marine biology. She's just a freshman this year and I'm helping her with an English assignment."

She plopped down on the twin bed without the slightest hint of awkwardness. Rowan, on the other hand, now realized he'd never been alone in a bedroom with her. Funny how his thoughts immediately ran to a fantasy-dream scenario. He told himself it didn't help that she'd been the one to suggest he play her devoted boyfriend on this trip.

How far did she intend this farce to go and would fake kissing also be involved?

"So...do *they* think we're dating?" He hooked a thumb toward the door.

"Oh no, I've already told Charlotte all about you. She knows you're my neighbor and good friend. You can't be the random doctor I'm dating. At least, you won't have to pretend around them."

She took his hand and pulled him down beside her on the bed.

Obviously, this situation did not affect her in the same way it did him.

"I'm *so* glad you're here."

"Yeah." Rowan swallowed hard. "Me, too."

For a second, she simply stared in his eyes, her own eyes shimmering, and he wondered if...but no.

He filled the silent pause. "So, Mrs. Havisham is watering the Three Stooges and checking our mail. She came to the door with *two* shoes. We might need a new nickname."

"Oh! I almost forgot." She stood and clapped her hands. "It's the first Saturday of the month! Do you know what that means?"

"Free steak tonight at the OK Corral?"

"Close, but no cigar. Tonight is the *tree lighting* ceremony downtown. We have to go. It's a huge tradition and you don't want to miss it."

"I would rather die than miss that."

"Okay, smart aleck. Why don't you unpack and relax for a bit before we go? I'll get changed and let you get dressed. Nothing fancy, just jeans and a sweater. But it will be cold, so layer up under your jacket. Gloves, too."

"Yes, ma'am. One second, though, before you go."

She stopped in the open doorframe and turned to him. "Yeah?"

"How's this going to work, since we're going to be out in public together tonight? I assume this is opening night of our three-act play."

"Oh…right." She tipped her head, wincing. "I'll need to introduce you as a doctor. Hope you don't mind?"

"Rowan Scott, MD. Kind of like the sound of that. Boy, those eight years went by in a flash. I feel smarter somehow." He straightened and touched the glasses he occasionally wore.

"You *are* smart."

"Nobody ever called me stupid, that's for sure." He hesitated. "But you know, maybe you haven't thought this all the way through."

"What did I forget? Nothing important, I don't think."

Either she did not want to discuss this with him, or the thought was completely foreign. She'd never thought of the physical part of this fake relationship, obviously, or at least not the way he had been since the moment she brought it up.

He was almost afraid to ask, but if she wanted him to pretend…

"Only something huge." He cocked his head. "Can I kiss you?"

Her hand flew over her mouth and her cheeks pinked. "I… I guess I did forget something."

"I'm a thirty-six-year-old man and I usually kiss my girlfriends."

"It would be weird not to. I agree." She cleared her throat. "Well… I mean, is that okay with you?"

"Is it *okay* with me?"

"I've already asked so much. I don't want you doing anything you're not comfortable doing."

Was she *kidding?*

"I suggest in public we hold hands, and light PDA." He cleared his throat. "Like kissing."

"Yes, one hundred percent on board with that plan." She gave him a thumbs-up.

"Be sure not to slap me if I kiss you." Rowan winked. "Out of instinct."

"No, because *that* would be weird."

Then she smiled and was out the door, leaving him alone to decide what to wear so he'd at least *look* like a doctor.

Chapter Three

Twinkling lights hung from the boughs of every tree, lamppost and shrub in downtown Bronco. Lit garlands with accentuated red bells were strung from one side of the street across other. Poinsettias and small potted trees adorned every spare inch of space. All the local storefronts from those located in Bronco Heights to Bronco Valley participated with kiosks, local brick and mortars displaying window decorations, outdoor and indoor trees, wreaths and lights. They'd turned the entirety of downtown into a winter wonderland. Bronco at Christmas was a little like being trapped inside a snow globe. In a good way.

Allisson turned to Rowan and stretched her arms wide. "What do you think? Do we go all out or what?"

"You definitely do," Rowan said. "There's no denying it."

Charlotte and Billy had chosen to stay home, cozy and cuddling in front of their fireplace like a couple of lovesick teenagers. The kids were meeting friends, which left Allison and Rowan to wander the streets alone together. Ever since they'd discussed their first public event as a couple while sitting side by side on a bed, alone, her skin prickled with heat despite the freezing temperatures. Leave it to Rowan to *ask* if he could kiss her. She noted he hadn't asked if he "should" kiss her, just taken it on himself to ask if he "could."

On the spot, she'd agreed. He had a point. No one would believe them unless they put on a show. But Rowan had been through a breakup recently, one Allison wasn't even sure would stick. By all indications, though, he was serious about remaining free and clear of Perri, so Allison didn't feel guilty. They were pretending, but she could kiss Rowan anyway because neither one of them was cheating. If they had to kiss…well, sacrifices would have to be made. She was up to the task. It wasn't like she hadn't ever pictured kissing Rowan before.

Once, they were sharing takeout from the Chinese food place down the street from their apartment complex when he and Perri were on a break, and she'd almost opened up to him. She'd been on the verge of telling him that she wasn't happy in her current relationship and wanted to break up with her boyfriend. The reason? Well, she hadn't wanted to tell Rowan that the *real* reason was she didn't think she should be dating someone and picturing herself kissing Rowan. But she'd chickened out and thought it best to wait and see what happened between him and Perri. The following month, they got back together, and Allison was glad she hadn't said anything.

She'd ended her relationship anyway because despite his reconnection with Perri, Allison continued to fight her feelings for him.

She and Rowan walked toward the enormous tree in the center of the park for the ceremony that would start soon. Outdoor speakers were piping in music from *The Nutcracker*. They stopped at the Bean & Biscotti kiosk to order a hot cider for him and a hot chocolate for her.

"To us," Rowan said, holding up his cider cup.

"To our friendship," Allison said, to make sure he felt no pressure.

"Man, this is *good*." He then pointed to a makeshift stand. "Holy cow, are those roasted chestnuts? I didn't know that was an actual thing."

"Yes, let's go get some." Allison grabbed his hand and tugged him toward the street vendor.

She almost didn't see the man coming at her until she nearly collided with him. *Frederick.* He looked as he always did, his upper lip curled as if he smelled something rotten.

"Allison." He nodded by way of greeting, as warm and fuzzy as a colicky horse.

"Hello, Frederick." She must have squeezed Rowan's hand instinctively because he squeezed back. "I want to introduce you to my, um, my boyfriend. Dr. Rowan Scott. Rowan, this is Frederick. He's a good friend of my father's."

Rowan stuck out his hand. "Great to meet you, sir."

Frederick dutifully shook hands, but with his typical sour look. "I trust you are both enjoying the festivities."

"I certainly am." Rowan didn't let go of her hand but, with his free one, he went hand to chest. "I live in Seattle, so I've never seen anything quite like this."

Frederick, arms tucked behind him, tipped back on his heels. "As a doctor, you must be quite busy. Are you here for long?"

"I wasn't planning on it, but I'm having such a fantastic time. And I sure hate to be away from Allison for long. Maybe I'll cancel all my surgeries." He tugged her close. "I think I'll stay until New Year's Day, babe. I can't have you ringing in the year without me. That's bad luck. What do you say?"

Not for the first time, her sister had been one hundred percent on point. The man smelled divine.

"Oh, that sounds great. Yes. Uh-huh."

Wow, he was really turning on the charm and he'd apparently just called himself a *surgeon*. Oh dear. But, judging by Frederick's demeanor, he believed him. Every word, she'd say. Then Rowan bent low, tipped her mouth up to meet his lips, and kissed her.

Just when she thought she'd managed to quash that attraction to Rowan it came rushing back with a white hot fury. She lost her footing during the kiss, holding on to the lapels of his jacket to steady her equilibrium. A tingle thrummed through her body from head to toe. Holy Christmas!

He'd prepared her for this moment, but opportunity did not intersect with expectation. The part of the Venn diagram where reality met fantasy was stunning, and electricity hummed through her legs.

"Well! I guess I will leave you two alone then," Frederick said, forcing them both to come up for air.

"That's it?" Rowan stared after him as he walked away. "He doesn't seem that disappointed. Or jealous."

It took Allison a moment to regain the power of speech, so she simply blinked at Rowan, the *world's best kisser*.

Who knew? That was nothing like she'd imagined it would be. She'd expected Rowan would put in the least amount of effort required, a simple peck on the lips. And quite honestly she'd hoped for a little less passion so as not to tease her too much with what she couldn't have. He might not belong to Perri at the moment, but given their history that was temporary.

"Um…"

"I mean I guess he must not like you much," Rowan said with a shrug.

"Me? He doesn't like *me*. My money? That's a different

story. I'm a Taylor, so someday I'll come into a massive fortune. I bet he doesn't even know what color my eyes are. I think Frederick looks at me and sees dollar signs in my eyes."

"So, he sees green eyes instead of blue? He wants to whisper sweet stock dividends into your ear?"

Allison laughed. "Something like that."

"Not very romantic. What a chump. I can't even imagine basing a marriage on financial assets. My parents have been married for over forty years and they're still in love. When they met, neither one of them had much of anything."

"You're lucky. You had great role models. That must be what makes you such a great boyfriend." She waved her hand dismissively. "I mean for Perri."

"She doesn't seem to think so."

"Then she's missing a sensitivity gene."

"You're just saying that because you and I are friends."

"I'm saying it because it's true. And, thank you. After that kiss, I'm sure word will spread through town and get back to my parents. That's the main idea."

"You're welcome, but kissing you was not exactly a hardship." He winked.

She was saved from a response when people began to move in small groups around them. Clearly, they were about to light the town tree. Rowan held her hand as, together, they walked toward the event. A few minutes later, everyone clapped when the bright, colorful, blinking lights went up the length of the tree, and the small crowd oohed and aahed into the night. "All I Want for Christmas Is You" by Mariah Carey rang through the speakers and this year's Santa Claus went around handing out candy canes to the children.

"Should we walk around?" Allison said. "I'll be your tour guide. If you have any Christmas shopping left to do,

I'll have to take you to Sadie's Holiday House in Bronco Valley because that's the place to start."

"I still need to get something for my mother. She's picky. With my dad, buy him a tie and he's happy. My mother expects a much more heartfelt gift from her sons."

"Smart woman." Allison pointed to the Bronco Ghost Tours kiosk owned by Evan Cruise as they walked by. "My cousin Daphne is married to the proprietor. Want to stop by and sign up for a tour?"

"A ghost tour? How could I say no to that?"

"It's such a touristy thing to do, but what the heck? You are a tourist." She spotted Evan immediately and made the introductions.

She hated lying to Evan, but she presented Dr. Rowan Scott again. "We'd like to sign up for a tour."

"I'm a doctor, so I'm a science guy," Rowan said in full character. "But Allison is trying to keep me open-minded."

"Everyone should be. I believe in science, too, but that doesn't negate believing in some things we can't yet see or fully understand. Remember when we split the atom? Who knew, right?" Evan pulled out the schedule and flipped through it. "How've you been, Allison? Still living in the rainy city?"

"Yes, that's where Rowan and I met."

Rowan nodded. "I have my medical practice in Seattle."

"What kind of a doctor are you?" Evan said.

"A surgeon." Rowan straightened.

"What kind of surgeon?"

Rowan cleared his throat. "Um, a little bit of this, a little bit of that."

"So, a general surgeon," Evan said.

"Exactly."

"How did you two meet?" Evan asked.

Allison had never known her cousin's husband to be so talkative. She wished he would stop asking questions already. Rowan was digging himself in deep and, pretty soon, he'd announce he'd won the Nobel Prize.

"Well, it wasn't because she was my patient, because that would be illegal." Rowan chuckled.

Evan quirked a brow. "And also scary. I hope you never need a surgeon, Allison."

"Oh, me, too. Me, too." Allison laughed, wishing she hadn't thought to stop by. "Actually, we met when I moved into the same apartment building."

The truth. Always so much easier.

"Cool," Evan said. "Well, there's room on a tour next month. We're already pretty booked up."

"Oh dear. I might not be here by then," Allison said. "I'm glad business is still good."

Evan gave her a small smile. "Thanks. It's a bit hard to celebrate this year, though, with my great-grandmother gone."

"My condolences," Rowan said.

"No, she didn't *die*." Evan frowned. "Winona just kind of…disappeared. On her wedding day. She and Stanley Sanchez were getting married."

"She still hasn't been heard from?" Allison asked.

She'd heard the news of Winona Cobbs's disappearance from Charlotte, but assumed the nonagenarian had simply wandered off and would be located soon. Winona was known to be a free spirit and it would not surprise anyone if she'd decided to chase a butterfly just before her wedding.

Evan shook his head. "Everyone says she got cold feet and changed her mind about getting married. They say she must be off on her next adventure."

"But you don't think so?" Allison asked.

Evan shook his head firmly. "No way. She loved Stanley, and she wouldn't just leave our family like this, especially after finally reconnecting with her daughter."

"But… I heard she left you all a message saying she was fine," Allison said, remembering the latest gossip.

"That's true, but I can't help but believe something is terribly wrong. I sense it. And, yesterday, I got another message."

Allison gasped. "What did the message say? Did you tell the police?"

Evan sighed. "No. Not that kind of a message. Lately I've been having strange dreams. One was of a locked room, a pen and paper. A note on the paper read, 'Don't believe them.' I can't prove anything. But I think somehow she's trying to send me a message."

"Did you tell anyone?" Allison asked. "The police work with psychics all the time, don't they? Maybe they would listen to you."

"If I get more details, maybe I will." Evan shook his head. "I wanted to tell Stanley, at least, so he wouldn't worry too much, but his family talked me out of it. They don't believe me, of course, and, anyway, it would probably upset Stanley."

There was little worse than not having the support of your family. She should know. But Allison believed in the unexplainable even if she wasn't sure what it all meant. She wished Stanley's family was more open to the idea because it could give him some comfort.

Allison patted Evan's shoulder. "I believe you. And I hope you find her soon."

Allison and Rowan said their goodbyes to Evan and continued their walk through downtown.

"Do you believe in that sort of thing?" Rowan said. "I

don't know. Sounds like a lot of smoke and mirrors to me. Pretty far out there."

"I know how it sounds, but weird things happen in Bronco. Stuff that's sometimes hard to explain. Many years ago, when she was living in Whitehorn, apparently Winona had a column she called 'Wisdom by Winona' and she seemed to be able to predict the future. Strange, right?"

"That *is* weird."

"If Evan has even a little bit of Winona's talent for predicting the future, his dream might be trying to tell him something."

"Damn, I hope they find the poor lady." He elbowed Allison. "Hey, what would you do if you could predict the future?"

"I'm not sure I'd like it. Knowing me, I'd get the kind of vague messages that are open to interpretation and spend most of my days trying to figure out what they meant. Then worrying whether or not I got it right."

"I wouldn't like it either. Half the fun is watching the future unfold and imagining all the possibilities."

"Hey, good job on deciding what kind of surgeon you are on the spot." Allison laughed and threaded her arm through his. "I was worried there for a second. 'A little bit of this and a little bit of that'?"

"Evan sort of saved me there. I walked right into that opening he so kindly handed me."

"Maybe you should have kept your medical career more low-key than surgery. You could have been a family practice physician. Flu shots and annual exams."

"Boring. I think I kind of like being a surgeon."

"No wonder. In the medical field, I've heard surgeons are considered as close to God as you can get."

"So, every time you say 'thank God,' I'll know you're talking about me, and I'll say 'you're welcome.'"

Allison laughed and shoulder-checked him. "I think we should keep everything as close to the truth as possible from this point on, like where and how we met."

Allison stopped in her tracks because walking not far from them were her mother and father. They almost never came out to these events. Just her luck.

She would now have to pretend with the two people who'd known her for her entire life. They'd seen her lie before and fail before. They'd seen how she behaved with someone she liked, like a boyfriend. They were now going to watch her put on the performance of a lifetime. If anyone noticed a crack in the truth, it would be her mother.

"This is it. Are you ready, Dr. Scott?"

"For...?"

"You had a trial run and now you're going to meet my parents. It's showtime." She flashed jazz hands.

"Put me in, coach." He pulled on the lapels of his coat. "I'm ready to play."

"All right. Let's see if you can score!"

She would just have to hope they didn't strike out.

Chapter Four

"Allison!"

A woman Rowan thought could pass for Martha Stewart's fraternal twin rushed up to them and embraced Allison in a hug.

"Hi, Mom. Dad." Allison turned to Rowan. "I'd like to introduce you to my boyfriend, Dr. Rowan Scott."

"Nice to meet you, Mrs. Taylor. I've heard so much about you."

Rowan stuck out his hand and the much more self-possessed and apparently restrained Mrs. Imogen Taylor did not switch to a hug the way Charlotte had upon meeting him. She also did not remark on how good he smelled. That was fine. This whole pretend-doctor thing was messing with his head. Pretending to be in love with Allison came way too easily, however.

And that kiss! For a second, he'd forgotten where he was. The depth and intensity of his automatic reaction slapped him with surprise. He'd always found her attractive, and assumed she didn't feel the same way about him. But Allison wouldn't have reacted and kissed him the way she had if there weren't *any* attraction there. He wondered if it was possible for her to fake that kind of chemistry.

He caught himself alternating between guilt and relief.

Relief that at least this part of their charade would be easy if nothing else. He'd nearly made a fool out of himself with Evan. Maybe he wasn't all that psychic since he couldn't tell Rowan wasn't a surgeon. Allison was right. He should have picked something more familiar and relatable, like family physician.

He hoped he was acting aloof enough, too, like a real doctor might. And he had to stop cracking jokes because the real doctors he knew didn't have a sense of humor. Too much death and sickness in their field probably. There was a lot to consider in a lie this large, but he was up to the task.

Mrs. Taylor gave him a smile. "I'm sorry we missed you at Thanksgiving."

"I'm sorry, too, but I had that trip scheduled months in advance."

"To Europe, was it?" Mrs. Taylor said. "It's very philanthropic of you to give so freely of your time."

Except her snooty tone of voice and pursed lips made it sound as though she didn't approve. He understood. Only a horrible boyfriend would leave his best girl alone during the holidays. Were Allison really his girlfriend, he'd never stand her up for any holiday or family function.

Though slightly distracting, he continued to ignore the buzzing in his pocket. Earlier tonight, he'd been shocked to get a series of texts from Perri. She'd claimed to be worried about him, wanted to make sure he hadn't taken the breakup too hard. Wanted to know if he'd made any plans and where he'd be for Christmas. He had not responded. Let her wonder where he was. Tonight, there was nowhere else he'd rather be.

Until the moment Allison's father strode up to him.

"Thaddeus Taylor." He stuck out his hand and shook Rowan's with surprising strength. "So. You're a doctor."

"Yes, sir."

Rowan broke out in a cold sweat. Regardless of his age, this man's eyes were sharp and intelligent. He would be difficult to fool.

"I wonder if I could get your advice with a medical condition." He rolled up his sleeve. "My doctor said I might have early skin cancer. I'd like a second opinion. What do you think?"

"Oh my gawd." Allison clapped a hand over her eyes. "Please."

"What?" Thaddeus barked.

Mrs. Taylor tapped his shoulder. "He's on vacation, Thad. Why not let the doctor enjoy the little time he gets off?" She turned to Rowan. "I'm so sorry, dear. He just can't help himself. I'm Imogen, by the way. Allison's mother."

"Don't they teach you this in medical school?" Thaddeus roared. "It's just a *freckle*! Why waste my money on a biopsy?"

Rowan tipped back on his heels. He so had this. Recently, he'd picked up a little freelance work on data analysis of skin cancer in the US and surrounding countries. Skin cancer, especially basal cell carcinoma, was a bit of an epidemic. But on the other hand, if he said too much, there might be further questions he couldn't answer. Or shouldn't. The last thing he wanted to do was give someone bad medical advice. He had to sleep at night, after all.

Rowan cleared his throat. "Unfortunately, I have made it a policy not to treat friends or family. I would definitely get the biopsy, however. Can't ever be too careful. Skin cancer is a bit of an epidemic in our country but it's not my field of expertise."

There. He sounded very smart.

Mr. Taylor pointed. "All you doctors do is *specialize*. In

my day, you went to one doctor and he cured everything from the flu to a broken leg."

"Yes, dear. We know. We know." Mrs. Taylor patted his back.

"I almost went into family practice," Rowan said, giving Allison a pointed look. "Might have enjoyed that."

She bit her lower lip as if she were biting back a smile.

"You're coming to our big Christmas dinner, right?" Mrs. Taylor turned to Allison.

"Yes, of course, but I'm not sure Rowan will be able to."

"I'm staying until New Year's, remember?" He pulled Allison close. "Things slow down during the holidays."

"What? Nobody gets *sick*?" Thaddeus said, voice dripping with suspicion.

"Not many elective surgeries are scheduled, and for emergencies, I have my partners on call."

"That's wonderful," Mrs. Taylor said. "All of our family will be together this year."

"Family and *friends*," Mr. Taylor corrected. "I think Frederick will attend. He's invited."

Family and work colleagues. It didn't sound like a family Christmas to Rowan. Thaddeus probably made it some big corporate event, mixing business and pleasure.

If Rowan stayed until Christmas, he'd miss his first one with his family in years. His mother wouldn't be happy, but when he told her he would not be spending it with Perri but instead with his friend Allison, she'd cheer up. She'd met Allison once while visiting him from Whidbey Island, where she and Dad had retired. Not surprisingly, she'd adored Allison and pointedly asked Rowan whether she was single.

He'd quietly reminded her he was dating Perri so *he* wasn't single.

"Oh, that's right," his mother had said, as if she'd forgotten.

"Well, we should go," Allison said, taking Rowan's hand. "I have to get up in the morning and take the kids to school."

"Yes, and I have to check in with my answering service. Just to make sure everything is fine and no one needs any emergency doctoring."

Allison squeezed his hand and gave him a tight "Are you for real?" smile.

Thaddeus's eyes narrowed to slits. "A doctor's work is never done."

But he may as well have said, *I know you're lying and somehow I'll prove it.*

Monday morning, Rowan woke to his phone buzzing. Again. Groaning, because he'd slept on a twin bed when he was used to his king-size mattress, he located his phone. Perri once again, with no less than seven text messages, all expressing regret they would be apart during the holidays for the first time, hoping that he was okay. She missed him. On one text, she'd sent a photo of them in happier times. His heart still bruised over the breakup, he didn't want to talk to her. But if he didn't respond, she would keep texting until he did.

I'm fine. Wish you the best. No hard feelings. Have a good holiday and don't worry about me.

Her response was immediate: a smiley face, a kiss face, and a Christmas tree. It reminded him of the sweet side of Perri, and he already missed her in a lot of ways, but he was also tired of their ups and downs. She needed to make up her mind about what she wanted, and so did he. He was done with the drama.

He shut his eyes and tried to get a little more sleep but, after a few minutes, gave up. He rose, showered, dressed and powered up his laptop to do a little work. He'd have to log in a few hours every day as he hadn't taken the entire week off work. One hour into replying to work emails, he realized he needed coffee. He'd never been a big fan before moving to Seattle, but with a shop on every corner, he quickly became a convert. The moment he opened his bedroom door, the smell of brewed coffee assaulted him all the way upstairs and down the hallway. He went like a bear to his honey.

"Good morning," said Charlotte from the kitchen table. "If you're looking for Allison, she took the kids to school. Help yourself to coffee."

"Thanks, I will." He found the automatic coffeemaker and poured himself some in the ceramic cups lined up nearby.

"I've got cream if you want it." Charlotte pointed to the tray of sugar and cream she had near her.

"Thanks. By the way, if I haven't said so yet, you have a lovely home."

Rowan admired the kitchen's cream-white cabinets and stainless-steel appliances. Someone had decorated tastefully with dark brown accents here and there, giving it all a cozy but modern look.

"Billy used to live here with his first wife, Jane, but I've added my touches since then. This is actually our first Christmas as a married couple, and I want to make it special for Billy and the kids. The kids have had a lot to adjust to in a short time. They deserve a special holiday with all the traditional touches, but time is getting away from me. I thought I'd have a lot more done by now. Billy helps where he can, but the Bonnie B keeps him busy all day."

"I'm happy to help in any way I can."

"Was it easy to just drop everything and come to Bronco for the holidays?"

Ah, so she was probably making sure Rowan had a solid career and wasn't some kind of gold digger after the Taylor money.

"I'm a data analyst, so I work from home. I'll actually be logging in every day until my vacation starts next week."

"Are you an only child?"

"No, I have an older brother."

"Are your parents still married?"

"Yes, happily so, for over forty years."

"And where did you go to school?"

Charlotte proceeded to ask him so many questions, he felt a bit like a goalie, keeping each one out of the net. Yet he answered them all. It made sense that she'd want to get to know the perfect stranger currently residing in her home with her husband and stepchildren. Besides, he had nothing to hide.

"And how did you meet Allison? I've heard her side of the story, now I think I'd like yours."

The questions continued. And he was ready for anything.

"We're neighbors, of course, but I've been living in the apartment complex for longer. I moved back home to Seattle when I got my first job just out of college. When she moved in, I introduced myself and tried to be a good neighbor. We've been friends ever since."

"You're underestimating yourself. Allison said you practically helped her move in."

"It was just a few boxes," he lied. "I think her boyfriend at the time ran late."

"Yes, and by the time he got there you were all conveniently done." Charlotte made a face. "I remember Tony. He didn't last long, did he?"

"I'm not sure." Actually, Rowan knew the day and time because Allison had come over to cry on his shoulder. "But, yeah, she deserves better."

It was the first time he'd seen such vulnerability in Allison, who always seemed so strong and upbeat. It awakened an unexpected tenderness in him.

"I agree." Charlotte took a sip of her tea. "I'm sorry if I've sounded like the inquisitor, but both Billy and I feel protective over Allison. My father has given all his daughters a difficult time. He seems to judge us in a different way than he does my brothers. But for Allison, who was closest in age to me, it was tough. I blame myself for what she had to go through as a teenager."

Rowan was about to ask why it would be her fault when Allison came bustling through the side door into the kitchen.

"Brr! It's freezing out there." She slowly unwrapped herself. Scarf, hat, gloves and, finally, her jacket.

Allison's cheeks were red and Rowan had no trouble believing her. Were her *teeth* chattering? He resisted the urge to pull her in and share his warmth, but they didn't have to pretend here. She'd think it odd, and he didn't want to overstep and indulge his recent fantasies about her.

"You're both spoiled with Seattle weather," Charlotte joked. "It's probably going to snow soon. I bet we'll have a white Christmas this year."

Allison turned to give him her full attention. "So! How are you this morning, Dr. Scott? Did you find anyone that needed *doctoring*?"

He snorted. "Yeah, I'm sorry about that."

"I take it you ran into some people last night and had to put on a performance," Charlotte said.

"Both Frederick *and* Mom and Dad." Allison poured herself a cup of coffee and wrapped her hands around it. "But Rowan pulled it off. Like a boss."

"Barely. Somehow, I got the bright idea that it might be fun to be a surgeon. I should have kept it simple."

"Oh no! A surgeon?" Charlotte laughed. "You've got your work cut out for you now. If you're not careful, our father will figure this out."

"I like a challenge," Rowan said. But, yes, he was worried.

"Dad already asked him for medical advice!" Allison said. "He rolled up his sleeve and asked him about a mole!"

Charlotte covered her face. "Oh my gawd."

"That's what I said."

"I think I recovered quite nicely," Rowan said. "At least they believe we're dating, and that's the important thing."

"You two look so good together, anyone would believe you're dating," Charlotte said.

"Mmm," Allison said.

Rowan bit on his lower lip and wouldn't look at Allison. He happened to agree, but that was beside the point. Even with that kiss, and her enthusiasm, she didn't seem inclined to take him out of the friend zone anytime soon. It made sense, and this was probably him again on the verge of making bad decisions. Even if Allison seemed perfect for him. It had been a long time since he took a risk with a woman.

For the past few years, he'd been inclined for a sure thing, which was one of the reasons he'd made such a mistake with Perri. Sometimes a risk was in order. In business, risk was related to reward. The bigger the risk, the bigger the reward. He was beginning to think it might be similar in his personal life.

"Why don't you take Rowan out for a ride on one of the horses?" Charlotte said.

"Once it warms up, maybe." Allison shrugged. "What do you think, Rowan?"

"Sure, I'm up for a ride."

It had been years since he'd been on a horse, city boy and all, but he welcomed new adventures. Why not, if it meant spending part of his day with Allison? He wouldn't say no.

"Well, you two have fun. I have a few things to do." Charlotte rose, walked over into the attached laundry room, and dragged an enormous laundry bag into the middle of the living room.

It took Rowan a second, but he interceded as fast as he could. "Let me help."

"Charlotte! What on earth are you doing?" Allison rushed to help. "I'll do the laundry, you have to rest."

"It isn't laundry. This is how I hide the kids' presents. It's the only place they're never going to look."

"Brilliant," said Rowan. "You realize you already have first-rate mothering skills."

Charlotte turned to Rowan. "Wrapping presents is an example of one of those things I planned to do but haven't gotten around to yet."

Allison frowned. "I thought you were going to let me help."

"You're already doing so much around here. The least I can do is wrap presents. It should be simple enough, but my energy level is so low lately."

"That's because the doctor said your iron is low. You're supposed to be resting." Allison yanked the bag out of her sister's reach. "I'll take care of this."

"And I'll help," Rowan said.

Charlotte gathered scissors, tape and gift tags and set them on the coffee table in front of the leather couch. The room was toasty warm with a fire going.

"It's a good time, while the kids are in school." Allison dug through the bag. "Let's hurry. Then we'll go for a ride, and I'll make lunch before I go pick up the kids."

Charlotte sat on the couch. "Don't worry about Nicky. He gets a ride home since he has band practice. But you will need to get Jill."

"I don't know how you keep track of these schedules," Allison muttered.

"The life of a singleton is much simpler." Charlotte laughed. "I remember it well."

Rowan exchanged a look with Allison. He didn't know about her, but he was ready for a family and all this wonderful chaos. More than ready. Two people who loved each other and loved their children. Love multiplied. If only he could find the right woman for him.

He now painfully realized that he'd wasted two years with the wrong one.

Chapter Five

"Hey, for a doctor, you're pretty good on a horse," Allison said.

"I should have been a veterinarian," Rowan joked. "But what can I say? Mother always wanted a doctor in the family."

Allison was impressed with the way Rowan took to Nicky's horse, Thor. Because Rowan was so tall, she hadn't thought it appropriate for him to ride one of their smaller geldings. Thor was a seventeen-hand black quarter horse who'd been well trained by Billy's crew. Allison rode Jill's horse, Sugar Bean, who was an unusually sweet mare. Hence the name. Though Allison used to ride, life in Seattle did not afford many opportunities and it had been a while.

All morning, she and Rowan wrapped presents in front of a fire while Rowan made Charlotte laugh. She found it was colder in Montana than she remembered. It might rain in Seattle a great deal of the year, but at least they were spared these freezing temperatures. She'd bundled up for the ride, because even the bright sunshine wasn't enough to quell the chill lingering in the air.

What she'd really like to do was fold herself into Rowan's warm embrace. She'd discovered he was solid and strong.

Stop thinking about him.

Just because that kiss had rocked her world didn't mean it had done the same for him. He certainly hadn't said anything about their kiss. She'd noticed, too, when he'd pulled out his cell a few times at the tree lighting ceremony. Someone had been pinging him. He'd put the phone away without responding, which made her think it hadn't been work or family. It was none of her business but she couldn't help worry those texts had been from Perri, trying to get him back. Heaven knew it had happened before. But she'd decided not to pry and simply pretended it wasn't happening.

She hoped this time he'd stand his ground and realize he could do much better than a woman who didn't appreciate him. Allison hoped he'd learn from the demonstration of a spectacular example of healthy love between Billy and Charlotte. Those two were utterly devoted to each other. Even with a blended family, they were making their union work. This example of romantic love was what Allison wanted, too. Everyone should hold out for true love and a real partnership. Her sister had been through a lot of turmoil early in her life and deserved every little pinch of joy coming her way now.

Their horses trotted through the hills and valleys of the Bonnie B, a gorgeous green carpet below them. When they came to the top of a hill filled with lush evergreens, she stopped to look below at the sight spread before them. A bird rustled in the trees and a cow lowed in the distance. She felt happier and more content than she'd been in years. Coming home was turning out better than she'd imagined.

"I don't know if I would have ever left here," Rowan said quietly. "It's not that I don't want you in Seattle, because I do, but I mean, why did you ever leave this place?"

She wondered how she could explain her love/hate relationship with Bronco. With her parents.

"Bronco might be better for me if my father wasn't so strong-willed. I never got along with my parents. Especially not him. When Charlotte got pregnant the first time, as a teenager with Billy's kid, *I'm* the one who got sent away to boarding school."

"I don't think you've ever told me this. *You* got sent away?"

"Yes." She sighed. "I mean, looking back, I understand his reasoning, not that I agree with what he did. He's a very controlling person and when he realized he couldn't control Charlotte, he worried with good reason that he couldn't control me either. So, best to send me to a school that would monitor my activities all day before I got pregnant as a teenager, too. He did the same with Eloise, my younger sister. But I was never a bad kid. Just curious. The funny thing is, all my life I've been afraid to express what I want because as a kid I knew the moment I did my father would take it away from me. So now, even though I know better, I'm still afraid to say what I want out loud."

"You realize that doesn't make sense." Rowan's smile slid easily across his face.

"Yes, but I guess some things are ingrained so deeply in us as children that we have to work hard to get past them. In answer to your question, why did I leave? Well, the first time, I was forced to leave, and I didn't come back for a few years. I wound up following Charlotte to Seattle, and then when she left there, I stayed. Not coming back to Bronco was my choice. I didn't feel like I belonged here anymore after so many years. And now? This is home, but it doesn't always feel that way. Know what I mean?"

He nodded. "And Billy's kids? I take it they're from his first marriage."

"Yes, he was married for eighteen years to their mother."

Rowan whistled. "Whoa. Big investment."

"Billy has custody, but she sees them every other week-end and one day a week. Charlotte and Billy were high school sweethearts and they reconnected last year when she came home. Her dream was to be a marine biologist and she made it happen. She has a great job at the new aquarium in Wonderstone Ridge, though she's on leave now. It was hard being from a small town with the weight of everyone's expectations. Our dad never took it easy on her either."

"I know about weighty expectations. My older brother was the first to play football at our high school and he dom-inated on the field. It didn't matter how good *I* got. He was there first. I had to find my place somewhere else. It didn't help that he's extremely good-looking and good with the ladies. So, I became the jokester."

"That explains…a lot." Allison made a valiant effort at biting back a laugh without much luck.

"Okay, stop laughing." Rowan grinned.

"You mean that you developed a personality, don't you?"

"If you want to put it that way. I worked hard to be ac-cepted for who I am."

"Well, now I have to see your brother, because I think *you're* extremely good-looking. Show me a photo of him." She held her hand out for his phone, which he'd been carry-ing with him presumably so work could always get in touch.

Reluctantly, he pulled out his cell and swiped a few times then handed it over. "Meet my brother, Grayson, but don't get any ideas. He's happily engaged."

Allison snorted, as if she'd be insensitive enough to ask for Rowan's brother's contact information. She didn't care what he looked like, but viewing the photo, she was amazed at what she saw. A man who might pass as Rowan's twin looked into the camera with a wise and confident grin. The grin said, *You'd be lucky to be with me*. She knew the type. Had dated the type. Hence her single status.

She handed Rowan back the phone.

"Well?" Rowan said.

"It's amazing."

"I know." He shrugged.

"I mean it's amazing how differently we see ourselves than the rest of the world sees us." She hesitated only a beat. "He looks just like you, Rowan. Or you look like him. Either way. But looks are only one part of the equation."

He put the phone away. "Maybe you're right. I guess I got set in my role as second."

Rowan was that rare man who didn't realize how attractive he was. He'd enticed the likes of Perri, an indisputably beautiful woman. But she'd toyed with his emotions, perhaps realizing that on some level he hadn't believed he could do any better than her.

Well, if Allison did nothing else this Christmas, she would show Rowan he deserved so much more than he'd ever realized.

By the time they rode back, brushed and put away the horses, it was lunchtime.

Allison found Billy by the stove, heating up some chili. Beside him were sandwich fixings and condiments. This wasn't good. She was late to make her sister lunch, so busy showing Rowan the Bonnie B. She'd been caught up in talking about their pasts and getting to know each other on a deeper level.

"Hey," Billy said. "Caught her trying to make herself lunch."

"I'm not an invalid, babe!" Charlotte said from a stool in the kitchen.

"No, but the doctor told you to stay off your feet." He

plated the sandwich then reached for a bowl from the cabinet.

"I told you I'd be back to make you lunch!" Allison went hands-on-hips.

"Sorry," Rowan said from beside her. "I guess I kept her away too long."

"Forget about it," Billy said. "We want you to enjoy your stay here, too, and I can help here and there."

"But he really wants to check on that heifer in labor," Charlotte said. "Which I find…ironic."

Billy laughed and ladled some chili into a bowl. "I may not be able to pull my own baby out, but I can help with that heifer. She's having a tough time."

"I hope this isn't an omen." Charlotte made a sad face.

Charlotte was worried about going into labor early or something bad happening to her or the baby. They were the concerns of a later-in-life pregnancy such as hers. That, plus high blood pressure, high blood sugar and any number of dangers Allison didn't even want to know about.

Billy set the plate and bowl in front of Charlotte and tenderly kissed her temple. "It's not an omen. The baby is healthy, and we just need to keep you healthy, too. Remember, I can't do life without you."

Allison observed the love and tenderness before her as Billy and Charlotte had a moment, quietly whispering to each other. She glanced at Rowan to make sure he was also noticing this sweet display, but instead he was looking at her. Her cheeks blazed with heat.

Self-consciously, she tucked a loose strand of hair behind her ear. "Now that I missed making you lunch, tell me how I can make it up to you."

"Since you mentioned it," Charlotte said, "I wanted to

bake holiday cookies for the kids and I bought everything I would need."

Christmas cookies? Allison watched the Great British Bake Off on occasion and realized that she'd never be able to make it into the big leagues. She could do standard baking, like basic cakes and chocolate chip cookies, but anything that had to look like you could display it at the Louvre instead of eating it was not in her wheelhouse.

"You walked right into that one, Allison," Billy said with a big grin.

"Cookies? Well, I'm willing to try!"

"And I'll help." Rowan rubbed his hands together. "As long as I get to sample the product."

"Well, that's a given. You're the taste tester." Charlotte pointed to him and chuckled.

"And if you need quality control, leave some for me." Billy pointed a thumb to his chest. "I need to get back out there now."

"Go ahead, Billy. Do your cowboy thing." Allison shooed him with both hands and gave him a thumbs-up. "I've got this!"

Oh dear. She did not have this.

Chapter Six

"Confession time. I've never baked Christmas cookies before," Allison stage-whispered. "But how hard can this be?"

After lunch, Billy had headed back outside, and Charlotte had gone upstairs to lie down. Now, it was just her and Rowan.

"Right? And I've actually *seen* people bake them before, like my mom," Rowan said. "So, I feel like I already have a general understanding of the process."

Before she'd gone upstairs, Charlotte made it known she wanted those cut-out sugar cookies in different shapes and sizes. She'd bought all the cookie cutters. There were snowflakes, gingerbread men, trees and stars. Allison lined them and all the ingredients in a row on the counter. Rowan, bless his heart, pulled up a video on his phone and together they watched someone roll, cut out, decorate and bake cookies. The baker made it look so easy.

At the end of the video, they exchanged a look. While he looked confident, she was pretty sure her general appearance said, *I'm in trouble here.*

"Don't worry." Rowan fist-bumped her. "We've got this."

But as they mixed and rolled and cut the cookies out, nothing went smoothly. They'd forgotten to turn the oven on and then realized, after their first attempt, that the in-

structions said the dough was to sit in the fridge and chill
for at least an hour before being rolled. Allison sent Rowan
upstairs so he could get some work done while they waited
for the dough to chill. She busied herself emptying the dishwasher for the five hundredth time and shuttling a load of
laundry from the washer to the dryer.

When she returned to the kitchen, Rowan's phone pinged
with an alert, and she found it under a dishtowel where he'd
forgotten it. Allison couldn't help but notice Perri's name
flash across the screen. An annoying insecurity flashed
through Allison. It was entirely possible that Rowan and
Perri were communicating again, trying to work things
out. And here Allison was, drawing closer to Rowan each
day. If they were thinking of getting back together, it was
none of her business. She had to give herself a reality check.

"Are we ready yet?" Rowan hurried into the kitchen. "I
was looking some stuff up, and the rolling is a *technique*."

Allison nodded toward his cell. "You forgot your phone
and it pinged while you were gone. I didn't want to disturb you."

Rowan picked it up, looked at it, made no comment, and
slipped it back into his pants' pocket.

Allison held her breath. "Anything important?"

"Nah. Perri is texting that she misses me." Rowan pulled
the bowl of dough out of the refrigerator. "This is our first
Christmas apart since we got together so it's kind of rough
for us both."

"I knew she would regret breaking up with you."

Her heart had no right to take the nosedive it did. Rowan
was getting back together with Perri. It was just a matter
of time.

"That does seem to be her pattern."

"Rowan, I don't want you to feel obligated to me. Feel

free to call her back and I'll take care of these cookies on my own."

"Don't worry, we're baking cookies. I'll call her back later."

This was classic Perri. She was already regretting her decision to break up. They had such an unhealthy dynamic, but it wasn't Allison's place to say anything. Let him figure it out for himself.

This time, the dough rolled out much easier after being chilled.

"It's because of my newfound rolling technique," Rowan said.

"Riiiight."

She didn't know about his technique, except it was messy. The kitchen looked like a flour tornado had swept through, the dark wood floor dusted with white as were the granite countertops. They each also had a white dusting on their clothes.

After the cookies baked and cooled, it was finally time to decorate them. Allison had looked forward to this part. Charlotte had bought the icing, too, and Allison mixed some with green food coloring in a bowl while Rowan mixed red in another.

"This is going to be great," he said.

She wasn't so sure about that.

"I'm glad you're optimistic. The shapes don't look perfect to me, but maybe that's not the important part."

"How they *taste* is the important part."

Well, he'd obviously never watched competitive baking.

She iced the trees green and he gave the gingerbread men red bow ties.

"We're terrible at this," she said, thinking her tree looked like a four-year-old had decorated it.

"Speak for yourself. I'm rocking these bow ties."

Suddenly, he looked at her and broke out in a big grin. Clearly, she had something on her face. She'd been so careful, but baking cookies had turned out to be a messy ordeal. Already she dreaded the cleanup.

She rubbed her chin. "What?"

"You've got something…right there."

He moved close and reached with a finger to carefully touch the tip of her nose. Then his hand lowered to cup her cheek and stayed there, his eyes blazing with heat. The buzzing that went through her body surprised her because it meant the other night hadn't been a one-off. There was something between them and it thrilled her at the same time that it made her palms sweaty. Rowan was too soon off a breakup, and she didn't want to be his rebound. She didn't want to be someone temporary between his breakups with Perri. Their friendship was too important. And Perri was not going to give up until she got Rowan back.

But then Rowan leaned forward even closer and kissed her, and she forgot all her reservations. The pads of her fingers grazed against his rough beard stubble. The kiss was even better than the first one, tinged with more heat, maybe because they were alone. He pressed into her, putting his entire body into the kiss, but then suddenly broke it off.

"I'm sorry—"

There was nothing to do but kiss him back, and show him how *not sorry* she was, so Allison grabbed him by the shirt lapels and pulled him back to her lips. This kiss was hers and hers alone, an exploration of Rowan's gorgeous mouth. He did not disappoint.

When they came up for air, he brought her hand to his lips. "What are we doing?"

"I'm not sure, but I don't want to stop."

"This is bananas, but it also feels so…perfect. Why is that?"

She didn't want to say it out loud, but maybe because they were trapped in the small-town holiday festivities and the warmth and love of the Abernathy household. Maybe Charlotte and Billy had infected them. If so, she didn't want any medicine.

"It smells delicious down here!"

Charlotte's bright voice startled Allison and she stepped back. Only then did she realize how close she and Rowan had been standing.

"Thanks," Rowan said. "Our first time baking and I think we nailed it."

Charlotte muffled a laugh. "Your first time *baking*?"

"Christmas cookies, anyway," Rowan explained. "I baked a cake once, but that was easy. It came out of a box."

Allison spread her hands out to indicate the tray of stars, trees and gingerbread shapes. "Our best effort."

"I bet they taste great," Charlotte said. "The kids will be pleased."

"I better get upstairs and log into work for a few more hours. Don't clean up the kitchen without me." Rowan grabbed a tree cookie and took a bite.

As he left, he brushed his fingers against Allison's. She nearly swooned.

"Wow," Charlotte said after Rowan left the room.

"What?" Allison got busy wiping the countertops. "I'm sorry we made such a mess, but I'll start cleaning now. Soon it will be time to pick up the kids. And what are you doing down here, anyway? Didn't Billy tell you to rest?"

"I had enough rest, and I wanted some tea." Charlotte grabbed a mug and a tea bag. "So, you and Rowan? You didn't tell me you two were a thing. When did that happen?"

Allison sighed. "It *didn't* happen."

"Liar. You can't fool me. You two were standing awfully close. Why do you think I spoke so loudly when I walked in? I had to announce myself because you two were really into it."

Allison shrugged. "It's just one of those things. I blame you and Billy. You're lovesick and it's spreading."

Charlotte laughed. "Rowan's very good-looking and so funny. I wouldn't blame you for crushing on him."

"Right? But the thing is, we're friends, and he's just out of a long-term relationship. Granted, it's an unhealthy one and apparently they just broke up, again, but—"

"But *what*? It sounds like he's free and clear."

"You don't understand. He's said that before, but they always get back together."

Still, they'd never been free at the same time...except for now.

"Sometimes it's all about timing," Charlotte said. "When someone is worth waiting for, you do it."

"It's just physical. And there's no way I'm having a fling with him."

"Yeah, you don't want a *fling*. You and me?" She waved a finger between them. "We're too old for flings."

"Speak for yourself," Allison snorted. "And you're not too old, you're too *pregnant*!"

"I'm too in love." She smiled with obvious satisfaction.

"I'd be lying to say that I'm not ready to settle down and have kids before it's too late for me. But it has to be right. At this point, I don't want to waste any time chasing someone who isn't serious."

"And how does Rowan feel about settling down? Isn't he about your age?"

"Yes, and we haven't really talked about that. I always

got the feeling he was far more invested in a relationship with his ex than she was. She's someone who sees how good and kind he is, and takes full advantage of his forgiving nature."

"I see." Charlotte smirked from behind her mug of tea. "It sounds like you need to *save* him from her."

Thankfully, Allison had a good reason to avoid the rest of this conversation. "Oh my goodness, look at the time! It's time for me to make you a snack."

"Way to avoid the subject."

"I'm just busy, busy, busy. Not avoiding you or anything." She pulled out the cutting board and sliced some cheese to have with crackers. "Have y'all decided on a name for the baby yet?"

"Honestly Allison, you can't avoid your feelings about this forever. This is what you always do."

And it's exactly what she was doing. "I'm going to take that as a no. I sincerely hope you're not going to be dilly-dallying on the name for much longer. You'll wind up with Beyoncé if Jill has her way."

"Okay, c'mon, Allison. Let's talk about this."

"Talk about what?" She looked up and waved the knife in the air. "My shocking inability to settle down, or the mean way I can slice this Havarti with my eyes closed?"

"Door number one, and it's not your inability to settle down. It's your fear."

"Ha! I laugh in the face of fear." She laughed maniacally.

Charlotte sighed. "I blame myself, actually. And Billy."

"Why would you do that?"

"We were stupid teenagers, and we weren't careful, so I got pregnant." She lowered a hand to her belly, no doubt remembering their first baby, the one she'd miscarried.

"Right, you were the wild one."

"I'm sorry that Dad sent you and Eloise to boarding school because of me. It wasn't fair. At the time, I didn't think much of it. I was so caught up in the fact that I didn't want to get married so young. But when I ran off, which was so cowardly of me, I left you and Eloise to deal with the legacy I'd left."

"Oh, don't be so dramatic. If I hadn't been so obvious and head over heels for Jimmy Lee, our father wouldn't have worried. But you know how it is. He just assumed I'd follow in your footsteps and forget the birth control."

"It just wasn't fair to send you all the way to New England, so far from home and family. I left but it was my choice. You didn't get one."

"I admit it was lonely for a while, but I got a first-class education and friends I still have to this day. It helped me get into a good university, where I made even more friends. It all worked out."

"Your education worked out, but what about your love life?"

"The search continues. I haven't found 'the one' yet." Allison shrugged.

"But maybe that's because you've shut down. You won't put yourself out there and tell a guy what you want. Marriage and children. The whole kit and caboodle."

"First, I would scare any guy off if I said that. And, second, *maybe* that's what I want."

"That *is* what you want, and you can't fool me."

"Admitting that I want to get married someday isn't going to do a thing but light a fire under our father to find me the right billionaire."

"He's the real reason you're afraid to admit what you want. You think he's somehow going to be able to take whatever you want away from you again."

Allison hated there was truth to that statement. Letting Rowan this close to her father was dangerous. Thaddeus could ruin this before it ever got started.

"Remember that guy I was dating a year ago? All it took was meeting our darling father *once* and he broke up with me. It didn't help that our father interrogated him over dinner and nearly asked to see his bank statements. He just couldn't hack the pressure."

She was only fake dating Rowan, and her father was already wreaking havoc and trying his best to make any normal man regret being a part of his family. If they were ever truly involved, maybe Thaddeus wouldn't stop until he'd scared Rowan away for good.

"It takes a special kind of man to handle our dad, that's for certain."

"Hey."

Billy's baritone voice behind Allison caused her to startle. Then she turned, saw the ax in his hands, and may have jumped a little.

"What in the—"

Billy grinned. "Char, your sister forgot what an ax looks like."

"She's been living in the city far too long." Charlotte chuckled. "I hope you're about to do what I think you are with that ax."

"Exactly." He leaned his shoulder against the wall. "I'm going to cut down a Christmas tree. Have I got any takers?"

"No, thanks." Allison held up both palms. "Not me."

"The kids aren't much interested these days either." Billy shrugged. "Jilly Bean is head of the decorating committee, but she's no longer as excited about hiking out to find the perfect tree."

"Did someone say something about cutting down a

tree?" Rowan appeared in the doorframe of the kitchen. "Because I'm in."

"All right! I got a live one. That's all I need." Billy turned. "Jacket, hat and gloves, city boy. Let's go."

Chapter Seven

Rowan trudged through the hills and valleys of the Bonnie B following Billy. They seemed to be headed into the outermost regions of the property. Rowan had pictured Allison coming along with them, which was pretty much why he'd volunteered. That would have been half the fun of the excursion.

Because, damn, that kiss in the kitchen. It was electric. He'd had to force himself to go upstairs to regroup, throw himself back into work, and ignore the fact that Allison waited downstairs. Ignore the fact she'd kissed him like she'd meant it. She'd held him tight, pressed her body into his, sending him the clear message this was what she wanted, too.

He'd like to think that you couldn't fake that kind of chemistry.

Don't make another bad decision. You're done with that.

He kept reminding himself that, somehow, when it came to women, he always made the wrong choice. Perri was simply the latest exhibit in the sad latest entry of his love life. He'd been asked to Montana for a respite so he could relax and have a small-town Christmas. That's what he would do. No get caught up in kisses with his beautiful neighbor and friend. They were not in a real relationship, and he had to remember this. Allison possessed the ability to truly mess with his heart if, when they went back to Seattle, she ghosted him. If she suddenly disappeared out of his life, she wouldn't leave a hole. She'd leave a crater.

It was a risk he wasn't willing to take. Couldn't.

"I didn't know you had Douglas fir trees in Montana," Rowan said to make polite conversation.

"We don't have many of them."

With an ax over his shoulder, jeans and a plaid shirt, Billy bared a passing resemblance to Paul Bunyan.

"The Alpine fir grow at high elevations and are similar to Douglas fir. Many years ago, my mother forced my father to plant seedlings for our annual tree, so now we have our pick."

Billy seemed like a good guy, but Rowan barely knew him. Allison had said a few things in the past about her brother-in-law. Now that he'd met the man, Billy seemed so down-to-earth, it was difficult to believe that all this land made him and his family multimillionaires.

They finally crested a hill and, in the distance, Rowan viewed a crop of narrow trees with layered branches, all growing close together.

"So. You and my sister-in-law. What's that all about?"

Far be it from Rowan to be anything less than honest with a man wielding an ax. Still, it just didn't seem appropriate to reveal their kiss-bonding over cookies when even Rowan didn't know what it all meant. Allison had been worried and skittish with him, but she'd also told him she hadn't wanted to stop. He was hanging on to that.

"Ah, she asked me out here to spend a real country Christmas. I work from home, so it makes it easy to pick up and go."

Billy narrowed his eyes and Rowan got the distinct feel-

ing he was about to be put through the big brother inter-
rogation.

"My wife said something about pretend dating?"

Rowan cleared his throat. "Yeah, that part sort of hit me
by surprise. Especially the fact I'm supposed to be mas-
querading as a doctor."

Billy quirked a brow. "A *doctor*?"

"Yeah." Rowan sighed. "You can't make this stuff up."

"Or, you know, you *can*."

"Ha. Yeah, exactly. I'll be making it up as I go. I'm going
to do my best but, quite honestly, your father-in-law will
not be easy to fool. I think he already suspects something
is off. It doesn't help that I'm a terrible liar."

"Being a terrible liar is actually a point in your favor as
far as I'm concerned. Don't let Thaddeus intimidate you.
You don't look like the kind of man who scares easily.
That's good."

"I suspect it's a requirement to hang out with this family."

"You would be right. My father-in-law tries to ramrod
over anyone who gives him a little room." Billy stopped
in front of what easily had to be a ten-foot tree. "I never
give him the room."

"That's good advice." Rowan eyed the tree. "This is the
one?"

"Yeah." Billy dropped the ax and set his hands on his
hips. "I'll need your help dragging the beast back."

Rowan slipped on the work gloves that Billy had handed
him earlier.

"You can probably figure out by now that I'm a little
protective about Allison. I've known her and Char for most
of my life. They've always been close. I remember Allison
always wanted to do everything Charlotte did, especially

when it came to the first wedding. All the decorations, party favors, cake, bridesmaid dresses. Very exciting for her."

"First wedding?"

"The one where Charlotte ran out on me." He grinned.

Funny, he didn't seem bitter. "I'm sorry to hear that."

"Don't be. It was painful at the time, but we've grown up. Getting married as teenagers wouldn't have worked out for us. Charlotte needed to achieve her goals first. Last year she came home to stay."

"You're a lucky man."

"Tell me about it. It's like getting a second chance at my entire life. The one I always wanted. There's nothing like falling in love and doing life with your best friend."

It sounded like the impossible dream to Rowan.

"I can only imagine."

"Look, let me be brutally honest. Allison is very special to all of us. My wife would never tell you this, but I will. She appears like this completely-put-together professional businesswoman, and she is. But at the heart of her is a young girl who got sent away from her home and her family for no damn good reason. Just…whatever you do, don't hurt her."

Billy stuffed his hands in his pockets and studied the ground.

And somehow that was a far more powerful statement than holding an ax. There was simply no need to ask Rowan not to hurt Allison. If anything, he stood the risk of having his own heart broken when they went home and resumed life as neighbors.

"You have my word. I won't ever hurt her."

Allison turned up the volume in the SUV. She had *The Nutcracker* playing through her Spotify playlist, and Jill hadn't complained once the entire drive. Good thing, because the music always put Allison in the mood for the festivities.

"How's your English assignment going?"

"I liked the story, but it's kind of sad."

"How so?"

"I mean, they're poor, so she cuts off all her hair and sells it to get enough money to buy him a pocket watch chain, and then he sells the pocket watch to buy her jeweled combs for her long hair. Dude! That's sad. She doesn't need the gift anymore. Neither does he."

Allison bit back a laugh. "The story is about sacrificial love. Selling what you own to give someone you love what they treasure the most, even if it means giving up your own treasure."

"I don't know how I can apply this to my life. Those people were poor and they lived in the olden times."

"Find a way to modernize it. But I'm not telling you to sell or give up something you love to give someone else a gift. I'm just thinking maybe you can use it as an example. A special and heartfelt gift, in other words."

Speaking of gifts, Allison still had a lot of shopping to do. Maybe she could talk Rowan into going into town with her while the kids were in school tomorrow. She wanted to get Charlotte and Billy a special gift and had no idea where to start.

In the past, she and Rowan had exchanged silly gift cards the way neighbors might. He'd give her a gift card to the coffee shop she haunted and she'd give him one to a department store so he could choose whatever he wanted. Too impersonal for this year. What did you give a man you wished you could get to know a whole lot better? She didn't want to overstep bounds, but this attraction to him actually wasn't entirely new for her.

She'd noticed him from the start. He was ridiculously handsome and so relatable. Always willing to help, expecting nothing in return. The men she'd met in the city who had Rowan's looks had always been on the make and had zero personality. Unfortunately, those were the guys who'd expressed an interest and usually asked her out. No wonder she was still single.

"Why don't you write about giving someone a gift but expecting nothing in return? That's sacrificial and goes with the idea."

Jill sat up straighter. "One time I gave Branson a belt buckle I found because I knew he'd like it."

"I'll bet your dad was proud of you."

"Yeah. He told me I'm his best girl."

"You definitely are. That's what I've heard, too." Allison slowed as they approached the Bonnie B. "That's the story you write for your assignment. How you expected nothing in return but gave your brother a gift anyway."

Outside the house as they pulled up was Billy, sawing away at the base of a huge pine tree. Rowan was right behind him, helping hold the tree down.

Jill jumped out of the passenger seat. "Hey, you got a tree!"

"Yep. Time is getting away from us and Charlotte really wants to get the tree up. We want everything ready for when Branson comes home. I picked the one I knew you'd like the best."

"For real?" Jill jumped up and down. "Yay! So, I did pick it."

"Yes, you did." Billy went back to sawing.

Allison walked up to him, shivering from the cold. "Um, need some help? I don't see how you're going to get that huge tree inside. How much are you going to cut off?"

"It's the same size we usually get. It looks bigger than you think. It's only about ten feet tall. I'm just trimming some of the lower branches."

"I don't know about this." Allison shook her head.

"You sound like your sister. Trust me. Thanks for your help, Rowan."

"No problem."

His hair was adorably mussed, falling down over one eye as it did whenever he didn't have it slicked back, which she'd noticed was often when lounging around the house. Today he had on his hipster glasses, the ones she only rarely saw him wear. He claimed he only slipped them on when his eyes were tired from staring at the screen all day.

Oh my gosh, she was so attracted to this man. To…everything about him. Even the way he bent to assist Billy, and then a few minutes later when he barely broke a sweat hauling in the tree.

This intense pull of physical longing was so…unexpected.

Allison followed them inside, watching as pine needles sprayed all over the ground outside, through the threshold, and trailed a path to where they propped it. There was a perfect cove by the staircase where the cathedral ceiling gave plenty of room. The tree was not only tall, but bushy.

This would be a wonderful Christmas, if only Allison could stop thinking about how she'd like to get Rowan alone and kiss the stuffing out of him. That wouldn't be smart.

Best to keep it friendly and forget that kiss.

Forget that it rocked her world.

Allison clapped her hands. "Who would like some hot chocolate and cookies?"

Chapter Eight

Three days later, they finally got around to decorating the tree. Allison watered it every day, but the trimmings were in the attic and she didn't want to bother Rowan much while he was working during the day. Billy had been busy with that heifer and Nicky and Jill kept forgetting she'd asked.

Finally, after Billy hauled every decoration down from their attic, the living room Allison had straightened earlier was in utter chaos. Boxes of ornaments, wreaths and garlands covered the wood floor. But it was a good kind of mess. She sat between Charlotte and Rowan and they munched on cookies and hot chocolate while Jill sorted through the ornaments and Billy went outside to talk to his brother Theo, who'd come looking for him.

Then it was almost time for dinner and Allison didn't know what to make. It seemed like all she did lately was cook, clean, do laundry and eat. Oh, and kiss Rowan. But that was only twice and, as she glanced sideways at him, she found herself picturing a third time.

"It's almost time to get Nicky from band practice," Allison said. "Then we'll figure something out for dinner."

"I'll be grateful when Branson is back. He used to do some of the driving for us," Charlotte said. "We were so worried about having a teenage driver in the house, but it came in handy."

"I'll get him," Rowan said. "I just need to borrow a vehicle."

It was almost too much. He could have disappeared into the guest room to work, or relax, but instead he was finding other ways to help her. Besides pretending to be her boyfriend, that is.

"Thank you!" Charlotte said before Allison could protest that he was their guest. "My keys are right in the bowl by the front door. The ones with the dolphin tags."

"And I'll bring back dinner, too." Rowan grabbed the keys.

"That's fine," Allison said. "We could always have chicken potpies for dinner."

Jill groaned. "Not again."

"How does pizza sound?" Rowan suggested.

"Yes!" Jill raised a fist in triumph. "Pepperoni for me."

"The best pizza is from Bronco Brick Oven," Charlotte said.

"Let me give you my card," Allison said, reaching for her purse.

"Nope, this one is on me." Rowan grabbed his coat. "Just ping me the address."

With that, he was out the door.

"Holy cow, too bad they didn't make two of him," Charlotte mused, gaping after him.

"Why do we need two of him?" Jill asked from beside the tree where she'd started to put up ornaments.

Charlotte smirked. "It's just an expression."

"Oh look." Jill held up an ornament with a photo of her and her adorable toothless smile in the center. "Here's one I made in first grade."

Allison joined Jill, taking a trip down the Abernathy family memory lane. She was surprised to see that Billy had wound up with all the sentimental ornaments the children made over the years. But then again, this was the home their family had lived in. It made sense for everything to be there.

"You'll be making new memories soon," Allison said, thinking of the new baby. "Charlotte and I were talking earlier about the name for the baby."

"I think we should name her Beyoncé. Dad said it's a girl and he didn't need the amnio to tell him that," Jill said.

"He just has a sense about these things?" Allison quipped, keeping it quiet that he'd guessed correctly.

Jill shrugged. "He knew I was going to be a girl."

"Or maybe he just hoped." Charlotte smiled. "It would be nice for you to have a sister. I know how much I love mine."

Allison's heart squeezed with love. She had missed hanging out with Charlotte. Their younger sister was busy with her new baby, Merry, but Allison would see Eloise soon. Even the idea of seeing her brothers Seth, Ryan and Daniel again was exciting. She hadn't realized how much she'd missed everyone.

"I've never seen my sister so happy," Allison said to Jill as she handed her a candy cane ornament.

"That's because she's in love with my dad."

Charlotte snorted. "She speaks the truth."

"And, also, he knocked her up, which no one thought was going to be this easy." Jill reached to put an ornament on a higher branch. "He's really good at making babies."

"Please, Jill," Charlotte said, and tears were coming out of her eyes as she gave in to a belly laugh. "You're going to make me pee."

"You don't think I know how this *happened*?" She turned, hand on hip, looking outraged that anyone would think her stupid. "I'm in Honors Biology and at the head of the class."

Allison was trying not to look at Charlotte because, if

she did, she'd start laughing so hard she wouldn't catch her breath. Been there, done that.

"Yes, and do me a favor and don't *forget* how this happens," Allison said, biting her lower lip.

"No worries," Jill said. "No glove, no love."

"I'm so glad your dad isn't here right now," Charlotte said, starting to wheeze with laughter. "But good talk."

Half an hour later, Rowan and Nicky returned with the pizza and they all dug in. Billy joined them, calling it a day at last.

"This is delicious," Rowan said. "The best pizza I've ever tasted."

Allison had to agree. There was just the right amount of cheese and sauce on it. Rowan brought them three large pizzas and one of them was a specialty chicken with white sauce that should win a culinary award.

But tree trimming wasn't over until, after dinner, Billy lifted Jill on his shoulders to place the star on top of the tree.

The rest of the evening, they all sat around admiring their handiwork by a roaring fire. More than once, she caught Rowan's gaze on her from across the room. And whenever a space beside her on the couch was empty, Rowan found a way to be right next to her. She told herself this was good because they should be familiar with each other if they were going to fake being in love around other people. He was simply doing his due diligence in playing his part.

But she was enjoying it far too much.

By the time he finished his shift on Friday and was officially on vacation time, everything was going so well, Rowan didn't want this time with the Abernathy family to end. He loved Allison's family. Nicky was another good

Abernathy kid, as it turned out, and on the day he'd picked him up at band practice, they'd talked music and favorite bands all the way home. Then, after eating pizza, they'd sat around admiring the colorful lights on the trimmed tree, Allison cuddled next to him.

She seemed to do that quite a bit these days, whether they were watching a movie with the family in the evenings or simply sitting around talking. Of course, he engineered it by making sure to always find a seat next to her.

Today, after work, he'd gone for a horseback ride with Jill, then come in to help Allison with dinner.

"All right. What are we making tonight?" He rubbed his hands together.

"Nothing fancy. Lasagna."

He noticed she had the noodles boiling and the meat sauce simmering.

"Looks like all I get to do is the layering."

"And that's a big help."

"You're not letting me do any real cooking. And you're not asking for my help around the house enough. What happened to turning me into Cinderella?"

"You had work, so I haven't wanted to bother you too much."

"Well, today is officially my last day until after Christmas." He raised his arms triumphantly. "I'm free."

"Time flies. I can't believe you've already been here a week. Want to go Christmas shopping tomorrow?"

"Try and stop me."

They worked in perfect harmony together, him layering the strained pasta, Allison ladling spoonfuls of hearty meat sauce, then they both sprinkled on the shredded mozzarella cheese. He did so far more generously than she did.

"Don't be stingy with that cheese." He popped her hand lightly and she dropped a handful in one spot.

"Hey, now see what you did. There's too much in one spot."

"Au contraire. Easy fix for that." He then dropped a handful in the remaining spots. "Can't really ever have too much cheese."

"I see you like lasagna with your cheese casserole." Allison smirked.

But the entire Abernathy family seemed to love plenty of cheese, because at the dinner table, it went faster than Seahawks' tickets during the playoffs.

After a dessert of ambrosia salad, they all filed into the living room to enjoy another one of Billy's roaring fires. This time, it was Allison who grabbed a seat next to him and cuddled in close. If he had it his way, he wouldn't move from this position all night.

Fair to say he was in heaven, so, when the doorbell rang, he automatically wondered whether one more person would change this relaxing family dynamic.

And he wasn't wrong.

Billy went to answer the door and came back with his in-laws in tow.

"Mom! Dad! What are you doing here?" Charlotte said. "It's late."

"Not that late! I can still drive after dark. I'm not completely helpless yet," Thaddeus barked.

Oh boy. This man was positively delightful.

"Of course, you can." Billy motioned to the couch. "Have a seat. I just made a fire."

"Oh, you're tree looks just lovely," Mrs. Taylor said, bending to kiss Charlotte's cheek. "What a great job you did."

"Thanks. Dad picked out the tree I liked," Jill said, patting her chest. "And I did most of the work."

"She's the head of the decorating committee," Billy said.

"Hey!" Nicky exclaimed from his perch on an oversize chair where he was playing a video game. "I helped."

"We just ate dinner and finished off every last piece, or I'd offer you some lasagna," Allison said.

"A doctor eating *lasagna*?" Mr. Taylor said. "Isn't that bad for your heart? It's filled with cheese and red meat."

Well, he just wasn't going to let up, was he? "I allow myself to indulge every now and then."

He supposed Thaddeus wouldn't be satisfied until Rowan walked around wearing a lab coat with a stethoscope hung around his neck. Then again, he *wasn't* a doctor, he reminded himself, so Thaddeus was right to doubt. The man had a razor-sharp wit, which he would respect if Thaddeus wasn't so mean.

Jill's eyes widened. "You're a doctor?"

"Anyway, guys," Charlotte quickly interrupted, "we do have some frozen chicken potpies. If I have any takers, we can heat them up. It's Billy's mom's recipe, and I know how much you love your grandma Bonnie's cooking! Right, Jill?"

"Sure, I'll have a chicken pot pie." Nicky looked up from his game.

"You just ate half a casserole of lasagna," Allison said.

"*So*?" the gangly teen said.

"No thank you, dear," Imogen said. "We've already eaten."

"I'm glad to see you two," Charlotte said. "How've you been?"

"More importantly, how are *you* feeling, dear?" Imogen took her daughter's hand and put her other on the large baby bump. "Oh! The baby just kicked. I felt it."

"She or he is saying hello," Billy said.

"Any names yet?" Imogen said.

"Don't pick anything stupid or trendy like Eleven or Twelve, or name your child after a fruit." Thaddeus shook his head in disgust.

"We won't," said Charlotte with what appeared to be a stiff smile. "But Billy and I haven't decided on a name yet."

"And the C-section is still scheduled in January? We want to be there," Imogen said.

Thaddeus was eyeing Rowan suspiciously, as if expecting him to add something to the conversation since he was a surgeon and all. He should know about C-sections and, of course, he knew what they were. Everyone did. A C-section meant avoiding hours of hard labor. He'd heard people talk about it as "the easy way."

"Good thing she's having a C-section," Rowan said with an intellectual nod. "The recovery should be faster and smoother."

Dead silence.

Allison was looking at him with an expression he recognized. Shock.

What? It wasn't faster? If so, why did people call it the "easy way"?

"Actually, dear," Imogen said, not unkindly, "the recovery is even longer with a C-section. Natural is always best, but not everyone can do that. Don't worry, most people don't know this."

"But a doctor would!" Thaddeus said. "Especially a *surgeon.*"

Why, why, why had Allison asked him to pretend to be a doctor? Rowan thought his best response at this point was utter silence. He became a vault. Decided to take a vow of silence. Pretended to be a mime.

"Tell the truth! You're not a doctor." Thaddeus shook a finger at him.

"Thad," Imogen said. "Your blood pressure."

Thaddeus ignored his wife. "He's lying. Do you know about this, Allison, or has he fooled you, too?"

"No, I—" Allison said.

"You're always so gullible, that's your problem," Thaddeus said.

"Dad, *please*," Charlotte said. "Don't do this now."

"Thaddeus, calm the hell down. I can't have you upsetting my wife," Billy said between gritted teeth.

"Your wife is my daughter and I have three of them. *Three* daughters! You're lucky you only have one. At least Charlotte is fine now, finally, but we need to help Allison come to her senses. Even Eloise is starting to wise up. It's Allison who's still making mistakes."

Rowan cleared his throat, and stood, abandoning his brief mime career.

"Let me help clear this up. You're right, I'm not a doctor."

"Aha!" Thaddeus held up a pointed index finger like Hercule Poirot in an Agatha Christie mystery. "I *knew* it."

"And so did I." Allison held Rowan's hand and squeezed it. "*I'm* the one who asked Rowan to pretend to be a doctor. It's because nothing I ever do is good enough for you and whatever I want is deemed stupid and inconsequential. And you know what? You proved it when you even found fault with a doctor! I'm sick of it all. I make my own decisions and I don't need your approval."

"All I want is for my daughters to be happy and content, but you need help," Thaddeus said. "You make *terrible* decisions."

The words hit Rowan hard. He was the one who made bad decisions, up until the moment he'd agreed to visit

Montana. Best decision he'd ever made, despite this humiliation.

Thaddeus wasn't done, even if his wife was pulling on his shoulder, trying to get him to stop talking.

"You need a man like Frederick. If I talk to him, I bet he'll still give you a chance. He has money and can take of any of your little whims, whatever they might be. You'll never have to work a day in your life."

Now, Rowan was annoyed.

"Excuse me, sir, but I have a fine career in the tech industry and can fully support myself and a wife, too."

"But you don't have *real* money. Legacy money. The kind that changes lives."

No, he did not. But he knew that didn't matter to Allison, it clearly only mattered to her father. Rowan couldn't take it anymore. Whether or not he was a doctor was not the problem. Whether or not he was rich was also not the issue here. Not to him. One other little matter presented itself front and center: they still thought Allison was dating him and, right in front of him, were trying to take her away. The lack of respect to someone who wasn't *legacy*-money wealthy astounded him. This was insulting and nonsense.

He understood now even better what Allison had told him on the ride. Her father took everything she wanted away because he didn't think her capable of making her own decisions. So, as she'd told him, she'd stopped sharing her ultimate desires. This was deeply ingrained in her because this man couldn't respect his daughter's choices. They would never be good enough as long as they were hers.

Rowan straightened to his full height, happy to press his advantage in this case.

"See, the thing is, Allison can't date Frederick because she's engaged to me."

Dead silence again, this time accompanied by a small gasp from Allison's mother.

He didn't dare look at Allison, but if she looked anything like Charlotte right now, her jaw was about to come off its hinges.

Billy sat next to his wife, holding her hand, a wide grin on his face.

"What? Engaged?" Thaddeus roared. "Is that *true*, Allison?"

"Y-yes," she said, and Rowan finally dared to glance at her, still sitting on the couch. "We…we're engaged. There's no ring yet, but we're thinking maybe after New Year's we'll pick a date. I…wasn't going to tell anyone because… well, because—"

"Because we didn't want to take the attention away from Charlotte and the new baby. So, we kept it quiet," Rowan said. "I'm sorry. My fault, I convinced Allison that we should keep it a secret."

There. That made sense.

Truthfully, Rowan had shocked himself, too. It wasn't just the idea of Allison dating Frederick or his wanting to protect her from an overbearing father. For two years of dating the same woman, he'd hardly been able to think the word *marriage* in her presence, much less say the word out loud. That should have been a clue. Only now did he fully realize his mistake. He'd wanted to settle down so much, he'd lost sight of the big picture. But his heart spoke for him now.

Thaddeus was still scowling but, thank God, he'd been rendered temporarily speechless.

"That's wonderful!" Imogen reached over and hugged Allison. "Looking at the two of you together, I just *knew* this was going to be the one. Welcome to the family, Rowan."

"Thank you," he said, wishing it were real.

A few days with Allison and there was no doubt in his mind what he wanted was her. It was that simple and that complicated. He wanted her any way he could have her. Things would never be the same after this.

Not for him.

But she had no idea how he felt. He feared that he was falling in love with Allison and had no idea what to do about it.

Chapter Nine

"That's one way to clear a room," Billy said a few minutes later, chuckling. "Thank you."

"You're welcome. What can I say?" Rowan shrugged. "It's a gift."

Allison's parents left shortly after the engagement announcement. Mrs. Taylor and Charlotte certainly seemed happy enough about it. So did Jill, who'd already asked if she could be a bridesmaid when the time came. Did he feel terrible lying to everyone? Yes, he did. But the kindergartener in him wanted to shout, *Allison, you started this!*

Allison left for the kitchen with some excuse and hadn't looked at him since her parents' leaving. Rowan was in trouble, but he couldn't help himself. The reaction had been automatic, and he was already in survival mode. The lies just kept coming. He'd started to grow real feelings and the engagement lie had come far too easily. The problem: he feared he was no longer faking. Obviously, Allison didn't quite feel the same.

It was one thing to feel a magnetic attraction and pull toward someone, quite another to become invested in a real relationship. Eventually, they'd both have to go back home to Seattle and face their real lives. He had no doubt they could work as a couple if she gave them half a chance.

Just because he'd arrive at this point first didn't mean she couldn't get there, too. He was a patient man.

"You really didn't have to keep the engagement to yourself," Charlotte said with a wink. "We would have understood."

"I'm confused," Billy said. "I thought you were fake dating."

"Keep up," Charlotte said. "They went from fake dating to fake engaged. It's like a reality show I can't stop watching."

"She's right," Rowan said. "I was in survival mode after admitting I wasn't a doctor. Then it occurred to me that as far as Thaddeus knew, Allison and I were still *dating*, even if I wasn't a doctor. He was trying to fix her up with someone else right in front of me."

"Rude," Charlotte said.

"I guess I lost my head for a minute."

"Rowan, can I talk to you in here for a minute?" Allison popped her head in the living room and beckoned him down the hall.

"Uh-oh," Billy said with a smirk.

"Hang in there, Rowan!" Charlotte lifted her hands in the sign of triumph. "I believe in you."

"Thanks." Her encouragement might be a little premature, but he followed Allison into the kitchen. "What's up?"

She stood by the stove, hand on hip. "Are you bananas? Why did you *do* that?"

"He was tearing into you, Allison. It was hard to just stand there and let him attack you like that. He doesn't have any faith in your decisions, or in your ability to make your own choices. I had to do something. I told you I shouldn't have pretended to be a doctor!"

"Fine, that was my mistake and I'm sorry I dragged you

into this mess. But…geez, now everything is so much more complicated. You heard Jill! She wants to be a bridesmaid." Allison covered her eyes.

Rowan felt terrible about lying to the kids. "Maybe we can explain later."

"*We?*" She crossed her arms.

He touched his chest. "I… I will explain."

"I'm going to have to give you a pass, I suppose, because you don't know how things work in Bronco. By morning, the news of our engagement will be everywhere. If not for the fact it's Christmas, someone would already be happily arranging our engagement party. And that someone is my *mother.*"

"I'm sorry. But I just couldn't let him try to set you up with Frederick. Is that what you wanted? Should I have let it happen?"

His heart seemed to skip a beat waiting for the answer. If she'd changed her mind and wanted to hang with the old guy, Rowan would step aside. But he couldn't see that happening.

Not after the way she'd kissed him.

"No, of course not. But I'm used to dealing with my father. I can handle him."

"You shouldn't have to take that from him."

She nodded, acknowledging the truth. "It's true the fake engagement certainly saved me from Frederick. And that was the point of all this."

"You have to admit, Thaddeus is really going to give up on you two now. Nothing says 'off the market' like an engagement."

"I suppose that's true." Her fire seemed to lower from a boil to a simmer. "Not that I would know. I've never been engaged before."

"Me either. But I've been told by—" He resisted completing that sentence because he didn't want to mention Perri's name.

"By whom?" Allison narrowed her eyes.

"Um, Perri. She let it drop that one way to keep a woman is to 'put a ring on it.'" He held up air quotes. "And it drives all the other men away."

"I see. And are you doing all this with me to make *her* jealous?"

"Am I here with you in Montana to make Perri jealous? Hell, no. She doesn't even know where I am or that I'm with you."

"Because if she knew we'd just announced our *engagement*, I have a feeling she'd be at the door right now, trying to reconcile. Pulling out all the stops. She obviously still wants you, Rowan, given the fact she keeps texting you. And she'd be an idiot not to try to get you back."

He let those last words encourage him and put his hands on Allison's shoulders, drawing her closer.

"Listen carefully. I would have never kissed you the way I did if I was still thinking about my ex. Fact is, I haven't thought of her once."

She gave him a little smile. "Well, we have a choice now. We can either ride it out at the Bonnie B for the rest of your visit, where we don't have to answer anyone's probing questions about our wedding plans. Pretend we're hermits."

"Or?"

"Or you go home and we tell everyone we had a big fight." That was his least favorite option. "Try again. *Or...?*"

She studied him from underneath lowered lashes. "Or we go all in."

"I'm all in. This is my fault, after all. I'm here for you. Plus, I have some shopping left to do."

"Me, too. I don't have anything for the new baby or a Christmas gift for my sister Eloise's baby."

Shopping wasn't the only reason he voted for going all in, but it was better than mentioning the truth. He wasn't done living this fantasy. The way he felt, he would never be done. They'd go back to Seattle engaged for real if he had anything to do with it. But he couldn't scare her off with the idea. It was going to be difficult to know exactly what Allison wanted since she tended to keep her real feelings inside. She'd already told him that. The question was whether she was afraid to say it out loud, or whether she didn't feel that way at all about him.

"Good. Then we'll go shopping as a team," Allison said. "And we'll handle the questions together."

"This also means we'll have to make an appearance on Christmas at the Triple T," Allison said.

"Your mother likes me, and I can handle Thaddeus. He's done his worst tonight. Everything else from here is uphill."

While he'd been working the past week, Allison gave Rowan the entire day to himself for work and only saw him when he came down for coffee, wearing those adorable glasses. But now it was Saturday and next week he'd be officially on vacation, so they had plans after lunch to head into town for their shopping excursion.

On her stool at the kitchen counter, Charlotte stirred her soup. "Are you sure this is all fake between you two? It looks so real."

Every time Allison recalled the expression on her father's face when Rowan announced their engagement, she smiled. She'd never seen Rowan so fired up and it was a side of him she liked. His was a righteous anger and he had a point. They were trying to fix her up with Frederick right in front of him. A lesser man would have simply pouted, but Rowan made his point with her father. He hadn't been intimidated.

"I assure you. I'm not engaged." She held out her ring finger. "See?"

"Maybe that part isn't true, but I thought you two were just friends and neighbors."

"We are."

"You could have fooled me. I know what love looks like. And unless he's a Screen Actors Guild member, Rowan behaves like a man in love."

"He's not. Rowan is a friend, and he was simply trying to protect me the other night."

"It was inspiring the way he went after Dad. Not many men stand up to him the way Rowan did. There's Billy and, well... Dante."

Yes, Eloise's husband deserved to be in that select group. "You're both lucky. A strong man is required to stand up to our father and put him in his place."

"And I think you may have found that man."

Allison shook her head. "I'm not getting my hopes up. His ex is still texting him and I don't like that at all."

"Hasn't he made himself clear with her?"

"He *says* he has. He says he's done with her."

But it bared repeating: he'd said that before.

"Then I think you should listen to him. Just keep pretending you're engaged, have some fun, and maybe when you go back to Seattle it will turn into something real."

"You know me, I don't want to get my hopes up and be disappointed again. Men have a history of doing that to me every time I start to get invested."

"Maybe he'll be different. You know what you could do?"

"What?"

Advice from her big sister was always welcome. For someone who was a marine biologist, so career driven she'd almost bypassed her childbearing years, Charlotte was living the dream now with her true love.

"You could tell him how you feel. Tell him what you want. A home. A family and children."

"How do *you* know that's what I want?"

Allison thought she'd done a fairly good job of hiding her desperate need to become a mom. She didn't talk about it because she might jinx it ever happening for her.

"Because you're my sister. I know you, and I see the way you look at me." She planted her hands on her huge belly. "This, too, could someday be yours. Well, not *this* one, but you know what I mean. I didn't know I'd have this chance again, but I hoped."

"And there was also Winona's special stone."

It was a rhodonite, a pink stone marbled with gray, on a silver chain. Winona said it helped the wearer achieve "emotional balance, cleared away emotional wounds from the past and nurtured love in the present."

"Which you could always borrow, by the way." Charlotte said, then sighed. "When and if they ever find her again."

"I don't know if I believe in that kind of thing."

"The point is, I let Billy *know* how I felt, and that I wanted to have a child. That I still loved him, and never stopped."

"Look at you, making it sound so easy."

Allison could never be so open and honest. She realized that didn't make sense. It wasn't logical, but her heart had a mind of its own. It seemed to believe the moment she expressed what she wanted it would be ripped from her. It wasn't true, of course. Thaddeus couldn't take her desire for a baby away from her. No one could.

"Are you ready?"

She turned to find Rowan behind her, wearing those sexy hipster glasses, his hair flopping down over one side of his brow. Holy Christmas! How did he manage to be more attractive to her each day? Of course she'd always found him attractive but her heart had never fluttered before when he walked in the room.

"Yes, let me just get my coat."

"How are you feeling, Charlotte?" Rowan said. "Can I get you something before we take off?"

"Nothing for me, thanks. And, by the way, the kids won't be home for dinner. It's their night with Jane. So, if you two want to stay out, that's fine with me. Billy will reheat chicken potpies for us. You two deserve a break."

"Is this your way of telling me you want some alone time with Billy?" Allison said.

"Well…" Charlotte answered with a silly lovesick smile. "Before long, we'll be parents and it's going to be about our baby twenty-four-seven. I'm counting the days I have left with him all to myself."

"Say no more." Rowan held up a palm. "I'll keep Allison out as long as possible. I'd like to have dinner with my affianced anyway."

"And take a coat and gloves, city boy!" Charlotte said. "It might actually snow today."

Allison finger-waved goodbye from the front door as she grabbed the keys to Charlotte's SUV from the bowl. Rowan joined her at the door and she quickly led him outside. Sliding into the driver's seat, she smiled at him as he buckled in, started the engine, and then drove them into town.

"We'll start in Bronco Heights, and then later we can drive over to Bronco Valley. First stop. The Hey, Baby store." She pulled over. "I need something for my nieces."

"Okay, and while you're in there, mind if I get myself a pair of boots over there?" He pointed down the street to the artsy window display of cowboy boots with elves popping out of them, straw hats covered in red and green bandannas, and sparkly belt buckles.

"Okay, see you back here when you're done."

Inside Hey, Baby, the adorable displays of baby clothes overwhelmed Allison. She would like to say it was due to the embarrassment of riches. So many choices. The truth was, her empty womb leapt with joy at the possibilities. Just walking in here gave her uterus false hope.

"Hi, there! Can I help you find something?" the clerk, Lisa, someone Allison vaguely recognized as being a friend to her cousin Daphne, asked. "Oh, Allison. How've you been?"

"Good. Absolutely great!" Allison said with false bravado. *Fake it 'til you make it.*

"Oh my goodness!" Lisa said. "Are you expecting, too?"

Why? Do I look pregnant? She bit back her sassy remark. "No, I'm here to get gifts for Charlotte's baby, and for my niece, Merry."

The clerk led her to an array of little holiday dresses, each one more precious than the last. Allison had no idea they made them this small. She could already picture little Merry in the frilly pink-and-white one with little ribbons. So precious.

She loaded up on dresses in all the growing sizes. "I'll take one of each."

At the register, Lisa rang Allison up. "You're such a great aunt. I'm sure someday you'll be in here shopping for your own little one."

It felt like pity talking and Allison bristled. Nothing worse than someone feeling sorry for her.

"I'm not sure I want children," she lied. "I've got a demanding career in the city."

"Hey, babe."

Allison had no idea how much he'd heard of their conversation, but Rowan strode right up to Allison, planting a kiss on her lips.

"Are you about done?"

Well, he apparently had trouble acting like a doctor but no trouble pretending to be her fiancé. He was quite gifted at this, actually. Almost like he'd done it before.

"Just paying right now."

"I'm Rowan Scott, Allison's fiancé." Rowan offered his hand. "Nice to meet you."

"You're engaged? I hadn't heard! Congratulations."

"Thank you," Allison said, handing over her credit card.

Lisa accepted it, then practically bent over backward, presumably to catch a glimpse of her ring. Allison took pity on her acrobatics. If she kept twisting and turning like that, she might injure herself. This was so irritating.

"We don't have a ring yet," Allison said.

"It's very new," Rowan said. "In fact, we should do something about that today."

"Sure." Allison gathered her purchases. "Very nice seeing you again. Merry Christmas."

"Merry Christmas!" Lisa called out.

Rowan held open the door for her. "Where to next?"

His enthusiasm was infectious, she'd give him that.

"I just realized something. You really love Christmas, don't you?"

"What's not to love?" Rowan grinned. "Parties, gifts, food. Candy canes. Hot chocolate. Santa Claus."

"Santa Claus?"

Hand to his chest, he feigned shock. "Don't tell me you don't believe in the man."

"Okay, I won't tell you," she deadpanned. "But my older brother once told me that our parents were Santa Claus. I think I was eight."

"He ruined it for you."

"It would have happened sooner or later."

"Some people tell their kids straight off that they're Santa Claus because they don't like lying to them. But I think there's something really magical about the myth. Good for the imagination. I'm going to tell my children about Santa Claus. The minute they ask Santa for a car, I figure that's time to fess up."

Allison was a bit stunned at how easily he talked about having children, as if he never doubted the possibility.

"Seems like a reasonable compromise."

"Hey, is everything okay?" Rowan took her hand. "You seem a little off. Irritated, maybe."

"It's just..." She blew out a breath, trying to find a way to put her feelings into words. "The store clerk. She tried to make me feel better about not having a baby. As if because my sisters are having babies, that means I should rush to do the same."

"Right. It's not a race."

"Well, not for you men it isn't."

"Do you want to have kids?"

They'd never talked about this before, but why would they? It was the type of conversation one had with a boyfriend or significant other. And that meant that if they were playing at being engaged, they should talk about it.

"Kids?" Allison cleared her throat. "I'm not sure. I mean... yeah, probably."

"Is this one of those things you're afraid to admit out loud?" He cocked his head.

Bingo! How did he know this when most of her ex-boyfriends had been eternally clueless about Allison? She blamed herself because she hadn't been exactly open with them, unwilling to risk too much. Rowan made it easy to admit the truth. Whether it was because they were just playing at this or because it was just the ease she felt around him, she didn't know.

A safe answer involved changing the subject.

"Since you love Christmas, I know exactly where to take you next."

Chapter Ten

"Sadie's Holiday House is always a favorite." She pointed in the direction of the shop. "It's Christmas year-round in there. Charlotte and I used to love that place. An old friend took over and I haven't been in there for a while."

"Sounds like the place I need."

They'd finished their shopping in Bronco Heights, and Allison was eager to introduce Rowan to her favorite stores in Bronco Valley, not to mention some of her favorite places to grab a bite. But even she was shocked at the speed of the town gossip mill! They were offered congratulations by no less than three couples on their way to the shop a few feet next door.

"See what I mean?" Allison said. "You can't keep a secret around here."

"You're right. Word gets around fast. But everyone is being so nice, don't you think?"

"You won't find too many mean folks in Bronco, that's for sure."

The display window at Sadie's Holiday House was themed on "The Twelve Days of Christmas," with twelve wreaths decorated in the gift of each day. There were little drummer figurines and instruments in one, another decorated with five large golden rings, and so on. A chalkboard hanging on the door denoted the countdown to Christmas.

Rowan held the door open, chimes sounding like sleigh bells ringing out. Allison walked inside, immediately assaulted with the aromatic smells of cinnamon and pine, two of her favorite scents. "White Christmas" piped through the store's speakers. Surrounding them were ornaments, artificial trees, wreaths, snow globes and even some jewelry under a clear display case. The store of her youth was now even better than her memory served.

Last year, Charlotte had informed Allison that the new owner, who happened to be her old grade school classmate, Sadie Chamberlin, had married Sullivan Grainger on Christmas Day. She was the same bubbly girl Allison remembered, all grown up, with wavy blond hair and dark eyes. Sadie Grainger now.

"Allison! I haven't seen you in ages! Welcome back to Sadie's Holiday House, and Merry Christmas!"

"Merry Christmas. I've been wanting to congratulate you in person on your wedding. Charlotte told me all about it."

"I got your gift all the way from Seattle right after the holidays. That was kind of you. Had I known you were in town, you would have also been invited."

Just like Sadie, who never wanted to leave anyone out of the fun.

"I didn't stay long last year," Allison said.

"How do you like city life?"

"Love it." She hooked a thumb at Rowan and the lie slid out of her mouth easily. "This is my fiancé, Rowan Scott."

The problem with all this pretend was how much she wished it were true. Lying had become as effortless as breathing.

Sadie smiled at Rowan. "Nice to meet you. You're both visiting?"

"I'm also from Seattle," Rowan said. "And I left my shopping to the last minute, as usual."

"Let's see the ring!" Sadie said cheerfully.

Allison sighed. "Oh, we haven't—"

Rowan piped up. "Actually, that's sort of what I'm here about. I got so excited, I asked her to marry me without a ring! Can you believe it? I'm *lucky* she said yes!"

"I can't see anyone saying no to you," Sadie said with a laugh, an obvious glint of male appreciation in her eyes.

Her thoughts echoed Allison's own. *How in the world is this guy still single?*

Allison would unwrap this mystery tonight. After all, Perri had been in the picture for only two years.

"Do you by chance have any rings we could see?" Rowan took Allison's hand and squeezed it.

"Rowan, I—" Allison said.

Sadie interrupted. "No diamonds in here, I'm sorry to say. But we have some beautiful vintage pieces, if you're interested in taking a look."

"I'll buy you a diamond when we get back to Seattle. I have contacts with some conflict-free diamond jewelers back home. But you need something for now." He followed Sadie to the glassed-in display case.

Allison stared at the case, dumbfounded. Was this really happening? No. It was all pretend. A show. But, seriously, Rowan was taking this farther than she'd imagined. It wasn't necessary to buy her a ring, for goodness' sake. She didn't want to think how much this would set him back. What was she supposed to do after the holidays? Give the ring back? Sell it and pay him back?

"Rowan." She pulled on his sleeve. "Maybe we could borrow one—"

"It's fine."

She should have considered asking to borrow one of Charlotte's rings. Allison had plenty of her own that, while not diamonds, would do the job when put on the left hand, but she'd left all those home.

Rowan seemed caught up in his shopping spree.

"Can I see that one?" Rowan pointed and Sadie brought out a beautiful ring, strands of roped gold with a yellow stone in the center. "What do you think?"

"Um, too *Game of Thrones*." Allison laughed and shook her head.

"That's what I think!" Sadie said. "Here are a few more that I think are more Allison's style."

Rowan reached for one ring after another until he held up a sapphire, a beautiful diamond-shaped stone set in a simple gold band. "This one. Don't you think? It reminds me of your eyes. So blue."

He reached for her left hand and slid it on her ring finger. "Hey, it fits."

Allison admired the ring then locked eyes with Rowan. Speaking of blue…his eyes were a deep indigo shade that reminded her of twilight. The dark piercing blue before it blended into the night. The kind of blue that—

Stop right there. This is bananas. Nuts.

But she couldn't stop. And now she knew why. She was in love with this man. He was more wonderful than she'd ever imagined. To think, all this time, he'd been across the hall from her.

"It's…beautiful." She stuck out her ring finger, staring like she'd never seen anything so sparkly in her life.

A thousand real diamonds could never replace this ring. It was one of a kind, sort of like Rowan. Just like that, a tear rolled down her cheek before she could wipe it away.

"Hey, what's wrong?" Rowan tipped her chin to meet his gaze. "Is this not the one?"

"Those are tears of joy," Sadie said.

"Yeah? Is that joy?" Rowan whispered, holding her gaze.

Allison quickly nodded, not trusting herself to speak.

In his eyes, she saw his concern for her, and her heart tugged almost painfully. The truth was, she didn't want to pretend anymore, but telling him the truth was another story. He wasn't ready for this, just off a breakup. He was just playing a part. Having fun. Because it *was* fun to put on a show if you weren't too invested in the outcome.

But she was far too invested. She didn't know how she could go back to Seattle and resume her normal life after having someone this wonderful in her life. Even for such a short time, sad to say it was the best relationship she'd ever had.

And it wasn't even real.

Rowan paid, thanked Sadie, held Allison's hand and, together, they walked outside. Only then did Allison realize, in her stupor, that she'd forgotten to do some of her own shopping. Good grief. She was practically in a trance, walking as if in a fluffy cloud, barely feeling her feet touch the ground.

"Hey, everybody! We're getting married," Rowan shouted.

"Rowan—"

He winked. "Got to make this look real. All in, remember?"

The next thing she knew, Rowan picked her up in the air like she was made of straw, lifting her feet off the floor, his smile wide.

Bystanders stopped to congratulate them.

"Good luck!"

"Invite me to the wedding!"

"Never go to bed angry with each other!"

Rowan set her down, took it all in stride, and waved. "Thanks for the advice!"

A truck passed by, driven by none other than Billy's own brother, Jace Abernathy. He slowed and leaned out the window. "Kiss her, you fool!"

"I think I will!"

Hand clasped on the nape of her neck, Rowan drew her close and kissed her in his spine-melting, brain-cell-dissolving way. He kissed her with such fierceness that Allison began to feel down to the marrow of her bone that something very real was happening. To both of them.

With his hands low on her hips, hers clinging to his shoulders, she was in another world. His lips were hot and insistent on hers, and she gave in completely.

Then the second most amazing thing happened in a smattering of days filled with incredible and welcome surprises.

It began to snow.

Chapter Eleven

The first snowflake fell on her nose. When Allison pulled back, Rowan's dark jacket was dusted by white. Flakes of snow were settling in his thick dark hair. She reached to brush them off.

He grinned. "I guess your sister was right about the snow."

Fortunately, Bean & Biscotti was across the way. Rowan pulled her into the establishment.

Two crossed candy canes clung to the glass window display and inside was a small, brightly lit Christmas tree. Ornamental red bulbs that almost looked like glossy red apples were strung along the counter between the register and coffee machines. The clerk wore a "Santa, I Can Explain" sweatshirt decorated with red-and-green bows and complemented by her elf hat.

Then the patron she'd been serving turned and Allison recognized her cousin Brandon's wife, Cassidy Taylor.

"Hey, cuz!" Cassidy said. "Brandon told me you were visiting."

Rowan blinked. "Are you related to everyone in town?"

"It just seems that way some days. But Cassidy is married to my cousin Brandon."

She introduced Rowan to Cassidy.

"What are you doing in here?" Allison asked.

Cassidy owned Bronco Java & Juice on the other side of town.

"Just checking out the competition." She smiled. "Now, can I see the ring?"

No doubt she'd witnessed the Oscar-worthy performance outside the window.

"That's gorgeous," Cassidy said. "Congratulations to you both. Rowan, you really got a good one, I hope you know. We're only related by marriage, but she's still my favorite cousin. I claimed her."

"I know," Rowan said quietly, almost privately, to Allison. "I'm very lucky."

"I'm sure I'll see you on Christmas Day at the Taylors!" Cassidy sang out, holding her coffee in one hand and waving goodbye with the other.

They ordered their drinks and the clerk served them in short order.

"Should we bring the kids home some of these cookies?" She pointed to the display case with decorative cookies, piped with icing in bright colors.

They were down to only a few of the cookies she and Rowan had baked together. No one had cared what they'd looked like. Nicky and Jill ate them with gusto and saved only a few for Branson.

"The kids will love you forever if you bring more cookies," Rowan said.

"You mean *you'll* love me forever," Allison chuckled before she fully realized what she'd said.

It took on an entirely different significance now and she wished she could take it back.

"Well, that's a given." Rowan brought her hand to his mouth and brushed a kiss across her knuckles.

Rowan found a table for them and they settled in, facing

the snow as it fell. To Allison, snow was always so much better from the inside looking out. Warmer, for one. Drier.

"Beautiful view," Allison said, cupping her mocha latte for the heat.

"Agreed."

But when she glanced at Rowan, he was looking at her. She cleared her throat. "So, Rowan, I was thinking that I don't actually know my fiancé quite as well as I thought I did."

"You know everything that matters."

"I'm not so sure about that."

"What do you want to know? Ask away."

"This is a tough one, but…why in the *world* are you still single?"

Rowan laughed. "You sound like my mother."

"It's just… I know about you and Perri, but that's only two years. You're thirty-six, so I know you have a longer dating history than that. And I wondered…was there ever someone special? Someone that you *almost* married?"

"Ah…you're asking about the one that got away. That kind of thing?" He took a sip of his coffee. "I could ask the same about you. Why are you still single?"

"I asked first."

"Fine. I'm definitely a one-woman kind of man and I've mostly had long-term relationships. Not a lot of casual dating, except for a little while in college. Yes, there was a girl or two who broke my heart, but I never asked anyone to marry me. I always felt when it came to that point, I'd know it, you know? I wouldn't be able to live without her. I kept hoping I'd get there with Perri, but if I'm being honest with myself, it was never meant to be."

"I understand. I asked because…well, sometimes you seem almost too good to be true."

"Obviously, I have my faults. I'd rather not list them

for you right now, but I can be messy and…" At this, he scowled a little. "I pout when I'm mad. And I stop talking…well, I'm working on that."

"That's very honest. And if that's all you can come up with, you're a prince among men. *No* guy likes to talk about feelings."

"I don't know everything about you either. You told me about boarding school, and I've met some of your family. But was there ever someone special? Someone here in Bronco?"

"No," Allison admitted. "When I was a teenager, I used to envy Charlotte so much for what she had with Billy. It all seemed so romantic to me at the time, that young first love. It didn't work out for me with Jimmy Lee, but I even tried to…now this is going to make you laugh, but I thought if it worked for Charlotte… I tried to get together with Billy's brother Theo. My father would have probably loved that. Theo had zero interest in me, however. He and Bethany are very happy together."

His phone buzzed with a text and he pulled it out then quickly replied, thumbs flying.

Allison couldn't help but worry it was Perri again. "Any problems? Work?"

"No, work is good. I've been working at nights after dinner, so I have more time free during the day. Then I had the catch-up day yesterday. Plus, it is always slower this time of year. That's why I took some time off, even before I realized I'd be staying until the New Year."

"You really don't have to stay that long. I feel so bad dragging you into all this."

"Hey, it was my idea to be engaged." He squeezed her hand.

"What about the plans you had to see your family?"

"Actually that text was from my mother."

"Oh no, is she upset?"

"She might be, a little, when I tell her I'm not going to be seeing her on Christmas Day."

"Rowan!" Allison lightly slugged his shoulder. "You haven't *told* her?"

"Don't worry. I'm phoning her tonight when we get back. She'll understand."

"She's going to hate me for keeping you away from your family."

"Are you kidding? She loves you. And this year Christmas dinner is going to be at my brother's house in Everett, just a short ferry ride for my parents. So, it's not like I'm missing my *mother's* Christmas."

"Do you get along with your brother?"

"I do now. We're just surprisingly different. He tends to show off all the money he earns at his marketing job while I live more frugally and sock it away."

"Like me."

"Got to admit, I was surprised to find out about your family. You struck me as a very down-to-earth, middle-class girl when we met. You're so unassuming, no one would guess the kind of wealth you come from."

"Money has never been important to me. Of course, I realize I can say that since I've been privileged enough to always have my basic financial needs provided for."

"Emphasis on financial."

"You know me so well." Feeling a strong pull of melancholy, Allison watched the softly falling snow outside. "I'm closer to my mother because at least she tries. She understands how difficult my father can be and tries her best to even out the playing field by playing good cop to his bad cop. But, unfortunately, he overrules her far too often."

"My dad tries to do the same, but I have to tell you,

they have the best marriage. A lot of compromise. Marriage is work."

"I never thought of it that way, but you're right. Charlotte and Billy are so in love, but there's no doubt they've done a lot of work to blend their family. His kids were not thrilled with her in the beginning. Even though their mother had moved on, with a new partner, they must have wanted their father to stay single forever."

"Yet she won them over."

"Yes, as you can plainly see, but my sister is the best. There's no way you can't love her. Just no possible way."

Rowan smiled. "I believe you and I think it runs in the family."

This was all so confusing. Yes, they were now putting on a show and doing a great job. But he didn't have to say such sweet words when only she could hear him. He could have also just given her a peck on the cheek instead of kissed the breath out of her.

"It's still snowing," Rowan said. "Good thing I bought these boots. You know, I still have a little shopping to do. Why don't we each go our separate ways and then meet back at the truck?"

"Okay. Then we'll have dinner at Bronco Burgers."

Rowan went in one direction, saying he wanted to find something for his mother, and Allison went in the other. Once she saw him go around the bend, she headed toward Cimarron Rose. She still needed a gift for Rowan, and she wanted something special. He'd bought her a beautiful ring, completely unexpected. No, it wasn't truly an engagement ring, but he was right in that the stone matched her eyes. It was such a sweet and sentimental gift, and she wanted something similar for him. But she had no idea where to begin and hoped maybe the proprietor would have some advice.

"Hi, Allison!" Everlee Abernathy, formerly Roberts, greeted her at the door. As usual, she was adorably dressed; this time in a cream white dress cinched with a dark brown leather belt. Brown leather cowboy boots completed the outfit.

"Hi Evy! You look amazing, as usual. I need something special for my fiancé."

"Congratulations. I heard all about your engagement."

Good grief. Allison rolled her eyes. "I'm sure my mother had it broadcast on the evening news, but I must have missed the announcement."

Evy laughed. "What did you have in mind?"

"I have no idea, but in the past, I've given him gift cards."

This year she needed something a lot more personal. But what? They weren't intimate—unfortunately—so it would be very inappropriate to give him the gift of her lingerie. She always thought that was a strange gift anyway, although ex-boyfriends swore to her it really was a gift to *them*. Cologne would be nice, but face it, he already smelled so good. She didn't know what he wore but she definitely didn't want to change it.

"I put some things together that we carry and might make good gifts for men." Evy led her to a gift section, but she didn't see anything that struck her as quite right.

Allison finished the rest of her shopping while she gave some thought to what might work for Rowan. A beautiful silk scarf for her mother, and a money clip for her father. Sort of a gag gift on her part, though he wouldn't get the joke.

He could never have too many of those.

And then she saw the gift. It seemed as though a neon arrow pointed at it. Perfect.

"Wrap that one up! I'll take it."

Chapter Twelve

Rowan circled back to Sadie's Holiday House once he and Allison separated because he'd seen the perfect gift for Allison. The ring felt like a gift of necessity, and she might think he'd done it to play the game. Far from it, but he saw why she might think so. But this gift would remove all doubt about his feelings when she opened it on Christmas morning. He was only waiting to see some kind of acknowledgment from her, a revelation and spoken words that this was no longer a performance. It was real, down to the snowflakes that fell on them like they were trapped in a real-life snow globe.

Allison was special to him and reliving his romantic history with her earlier had only put a fine point on it. He'd never felt this way about any woman he'd dated and yet, in other ways, she made him feel like a teenager all over again with his first crush. He couldn't stop touching her, couldn't stop kissing her, and he wanted so much more. Her mouth, those mile-long legs, her beautiful eyes. He was out of his mind with lust.

"You're back!" Sadie said when he opened the shop door and the chimes sounded.

"I saw something while we were here before, but I want this gift to be a surprise." He pointed to the gold chain with a locket in the shape of an envelope. Perfect.

A way for her to remember the time she'd asked him to pick up her mail but instead he'd visited her in Montana and fallen in love with her. He hoped when they both returned to Seattle everything between them would be different. The locket was beautiful and perfect, but as he held it, one side slid open and revealed a message engraved inside: *I love you.*

Was it too much? He understood that Allison was hesitant to express her feelings, so he couldn't play that game, too. Instead, it was time to reveal what he wanted, what he now knew he'd wanted since the day he'd first laid eyes on her. But beyond just having a good time as he'd initially fantasized, he wanted an entire future with her.

He was going to tell her before Christmas.

It didn't take him long to finish his shopping after buying the locket, so he took a minute and stepped outside to phone his mother. The call was long overdue.

"Hey, Mom. I have some bad news. Don't be too upset with me, okay?"

"Oh no. What has she done now?"

Yikes. She thought this was about Perri, no doubt. Mom was not a fan.

"I'm not going to be able to make it home for Christmas."

"But you spent it with Perri's family last year. It's our turn!"

Rowan winced. She was right. "I promise to make it up to you next year."

Next year, maybe he and Allison would spend Christmas in Washington with his family. They would all love her.

"Don't tell me you're working."

"No, not working."

"Going to *Perri's family* again?" The tone in her voice said she might consider cutting him out of the will.

"No, actually, Perri and I broke up."

A beat of silence and then she said in a cheerful voice, "Well, that's too bad."

"It was time. We're really done."

"Are you sad? You don't sound sad."

"Maybe at first because I feel like I've invested so much in her. But now I'm happier than I've ever been."

He considered how much he should reveal. The whole pretend-engagement thing sounded a little farfetched. His mother wouldn't appreciate the farce and might worry too much.

"Remember my neighbor, Allison Taylor? She needed my help, so I'm in Bronco, Montana, literally having a white Christmas."

"You're with Allison? That's…why, that's wonderful."

"Yeah, so I won't be able to make dinner at Grayson's. Should I call him, or will you tell him?"

"I'll let him know, don't worry. His fiancée is a bit nervous about hosting this year, so at least this will ease some of her tension."

"Why? It's just one less person."

"She wants every little detail to be perfect. You know she tries so hard to impress you. They both do."

Wait. *What?* In Rowan's mind, they tried hard to one-up him. Whatever Rowan did, they did it bigger. Last year, Rowan had sprung for a new water-efficient dishwasher in his kitchen. They'd renovated their entire kitchen with energy-saving appliances. When Rowan bought a Tesla to save on gasoline they'd purchased his-and-her matching ones.

"I don't know why she's worried about impressing me. You know me. I'll eat just about anything."

She chuckled. "It must be because she knows how important you are to the family. You're the lifeblood of the Scotts. Our comic relief when something goes wrong. Our cheerleader and protector. But we'll try to be fine without you this year. Just promise me one thing."

"Of course. Anything."

"Don't leave Montana without telling Allison how you feel about her."

Rowan coughed and hit his chest. It was as if she could read his mind, or the tea leaves, or some such thing.

Maybe Evan Cruise wasn't the only psychic he'd met.

"Um, *what*?"

"Honey, it's so obvious. The entire time you've dated Perri, you've talked about Allison instead. 'Allison thinks this' and 'Allison said that.' You did things with Perri, you *dated* her, but you talked about Allison. She was in your heart from the moment she moved into that building. Am I wrong?"

She wasn't wrong and Rowan didn't know how he'd never realized it before this trip. Maybe because she seemed like a far-away impossibility. Like someone who'd never think of him as more than a friend. He didn't know if this pretend relationship had been the clincher to make her see him in a new way, or if maybe this had been a possibility all along.

Either way, he'd take it.

By the time dinner rolled around, Rowan had walked from one end of town to the other, appreciating everything he saw. The snow was sticking to every available surface. People were scurrying by on their way to a shop or their vehicle. The air had a bite to it, a slight wind occasionally breaking through the barrier of his jacket.

After a few minutes, he saw Allison by the truck, loading some of her bags, and ran to join her. Throwing some of his own shopping into the back seat, he kept the locket in his pocket and close to him. He didn't want her catching even a glimpse of it a moment before Christmas. Timing was everything and this time he'd get it right.

"I hope you're hungry," Allison said. "Bronco Burgers has some juicy burgers but a little bit of everything."

Not surprisingly, the establishment was busy with many people seeking shelter from the falling snow. They were able to snag a seat in a booth, however, and, rather than sit across from Allison, he slid in next to her.

"I'll be right back for your order," the server said.

Rowan reached for Allison's hand. "I missed you."

She laughed. "We were separated for two hours, if that."

She thought he was simply pretending for the crowd around them. And of course she would assume that, since he hadn't made any effort to tell her the truth. None of this was fake anymore. Not for him.

"What are you having?" She flipped through the menu. "The burgers are flame-broiled and exceptional. I haven't had one of those in ages. And they're really known for the shakes."

He would like to have Allison on a platter, both for appetizer, dinner and dessert. But that wasn't likely to happen at her sister's house.

Behave yourself, Rowan.

"I'll have the same." He hovered over her shoulder, glancing at the menu even though he had his own. "You know what I was thinking?"

"That you want dessert?" She smiled and winked.

The way she'd said the words, it was almost as if her thoughts were running parallel to his own.

"And maybe even before you have a burger?" She completed the thought.

Yeah. He wasn't *that* lucky. "What I was thinking is that, for an engaged couple, we haven't had a lot of privacy."

"Shh. Don't tell anybody, but we're not actually engaged," she whispered.

"That doesn't mean I wouldn't like a little privacy."

"For...?" Her eyes were dilated and shimmering.

"To kiss you the way I really want to. The way I'd do it when it isn't a public display."

She bit her lower lip. "Given the way you kissed me, if it gets any hotter, I might explode."

"Yes, exactly. I *want* you to explode."

"Rowan. What are we doing?" She cupped the side of his face.

"Whatever you want. For as long as you want." He rested his hand on her leg, their knees bumping against each other. "Tell me you don't feel something real happening between us."

"I do, but I don't know what to do about that."

"Let me help you. Had I known you felt even a small amount of interest in me, I would have asked you out a long time ago. I thought you'd relegated me to the friend zone from the start."

"I never did, and I've always been attracted to you. It's just the timing was always off for us."

"I know, and I feel like I've wasted so much time. I don't want to waste any more."

"I understand wasted time. I'm thirty-six years old and I want...so many things."

"Are you willing to tell me what you want? Because I need to hear it from you. You've told me how hard it is to express your feelings and that's why I'm telling you first. I like you a lot and everything we've been doing since I got here is like a fantasy come to life for me."

This was exactly the moment the server came to take their orders, making Rowan wonder if their timing was still off. They both ordered burgers and when the server finally left, Allison turned her entire body to his.

"You asked me what I want. I'm going to be honest. Maybe… I don't know, but *maybe* I want a baby someday soon because I'm running out of time. So, if you're not interested in a family, that's a deal-breaker for me, even though, yes, I'm kind of crazy about you, too."

He did not hesitate. With the right woman, he was ready for everything.

"Sign me up. I love kids. For sure I want at least one, maybe two, but you know I'm a conservationist." Rowan wanted more even if he realized he might be pushing her too far. "And what else do you want?"

"I'd like to be married first, to the right man, of course. Not necessarily for me, but mostly for my mother. And as much as my father annoys me, I would rather not give him a coronary. He already had two daughters pregnant before marriage."

"And what else?"

"I've already said enough. What if none of this happens just because I want it too much?"

"You know in your heart that doesn't make any sense, babe." It was the first time he'd called her by the name privately. "I want to give you everything you want."

"I swear, you're too good to be true." She rested her hand on his knee.

"Nope. Far from it. Just wait until the Seahawks lose their chance at the Super Bowl again."

"Oh, I do remember. Wasn't that the time you didn't

come out of your apartment for days? I'd usually see you in the hallway every morning when you were on your way back from grabbing a coffee and I was on my way to work. That week I was so worried about you I knocked on your door for a welfare check." She seemed to fight a smile.

He was flattered she remembered. Almost as much as he'd been when she'd knocked on his door to check on him all those months ago. The next day she'd had a condolence fruit basket delivered with a card that said, "Maybe next year! Go, Seahawks!"

He'd smiled for days.

"I hope you know a girl doesn't just ask *anyone* to come out and visit her hometown and stay with her family. She doesn't ask a random guy to pretend to be her boyfriend. I asked you because I trust you. Because for me, you're... special."

"You're special to me, too."

The server arrived with their plates, and it was difficult to eat when they were touching each other every few seconds. She fed him a French fry and he kissed her, wanting a taste of her meal. They didn't have dessert, after all, because suddenly it seemed they both wanted to get out of there fast. He wanted to find that privacy he'd mentioned earlier and hoped she was thinking along the same lines. If their timing was good, Charlotte and Billy would be asleep since they were both early risers. As for the kids, he wasn't sure if they'd be back right after dinner at their mother's. They were sort of the wild card. But for Rowan, hope sprang eternal.

They pulled up to the ranch house a few minutes later. Almost every light in the house appeared to be off.

"Maybe everyone's gone to bed," Allison said, and they walked hand in hand to the porch.

Rowan mentally crossed everything. When they got to the porch, he couldn't wait another minute and turned her to him, bringing her in for a hot kiss. She responded and, before long, he'd moved her against the porch rail, lifting her leg up and kissing her hard and deep. She moaned and threaded her fingers through his hair. They were both wearing too many clothes, making this all difficult. Inside, he'd like to peel every piece of her clothing off. Slowly.

She pulled away with a gasp. "Let's go to my room."

Rowan would have torn the front door off its hinges to get there but it seemed her key worked fine. He was right behind her, hand on her butt as she swung open the door.

"Hey, Aunt Allison."

The light was dim, but he spied two teenage boys lying in juxtaposing positions on the big couch, each holding a handheld device. He would bet everything he had that the two were online gaming in the same world, a few feet away, speaking to each other only through the game. Obstacle number one and number two. The boys.

This was probably Rowan's punishment for having once been a teenage boy with only one thing on his mind.

Similar to tonight, in fact.

He'd never seen one of the boys before today but the minute he turned to face them, Rowan knew he'd have recognized him anywhere. He was the teenage version of Billy Abernathy. The lanky kid stood and did the obligatory nephew hug with Allison, an awkward sort of half hug.

"Welcome home, stranger." Allison patted Branson's back, giving Rowan a frozen smile over the young man's shoulder. "We sure missed you around here. Rowan, this is Branson, Billy's oldest. He's going to bunk with his brother while you're here."

Rowan offered his hand. "Rowan Scott. Thanks for sharing your room."

He was stuck on whether he should refer to himself as Allison's fiancé, boyfriend, or simply friend. Friend who was in love with her. But TMI for the kid who, Rowan knew, did *not* want to know what Rowan had pictured doing to their aunt only seconds ago.

"Oh, you're the one who pretended to be a doctor," Branson chuckled. "Dude, that was awesome. Nicky told me all about it."

"Not so awesome. I screwed up because I didn't know anything about a C-section." Rowan shook his head. "Turns out I'm a terrible surgeon."

"All I know is you stood up to Mr. Taylor and my dad was wicked impressed."

"Good to know." Rowan faked a yawn. "Well, I'm going to bed. We spent all day shopping."

"Yes, me, too. I'll see you two in the morning," Allison said and gave Rowan a small conspiratorial and wicked smile.

They were halfway up the stairs, him right behind Allison again, when Jill came down the steps.

"Could you help me with the essay for my assignment? I got an extra day, but I said I'd email it to my teacher tonight. I just want another set of eyes before I hit Send."

Obstacle number three: the brilliant niece. Rowan saw his hopes evaporating.

"Oh. Sure, honey."

And with those words, Rowan kissed away all hope of spending the night in Allison's arms.

It had probably been a bad idea anyway.

Chapter Thirteen

For the next week, Allison tried to stay away from Rowan, which wasn't easy living in the same crowded ranch house. She'd watched him slowly disappear into Branson's bedroom on the night they almost let their raging hormones get the best of them. Then she'd followed Jill into her bedroom and helped her with the assignment until it was time for bed. She'd wanted desperately to go to Rowan, coming so close she had her fist hovering against the door of his bedroom ready to knock.

Saturday morning, Allison woke to the alarm she'd set on her phone. She picked it up and, for a moment, simply stared at the words in confusion: food drive at the high school.

The commitments around here never stopped. She groaned and rolled out of bed, reminded of how busy the holiday season could be in Bronco. Everyone contributed in some way, and when she'd first arrived, Allison had been approached to volunteer her time at the food drive. It meant she'd spend at least part of the day at her old high school where it was being held this year.

It would be another way to avoid Rowan for at least part of the day. She'd been doing a fine job of it since the night they'd almost made a huge mistake and slipped into her bedroom together for a little adult fun. The moment had seemed so right, so perfect, but divine intervention had come in the form of three teenagers. At first, she'd been annoyed and disappointed, but it didn't take long before Allison realized what a huge mistake she'd almost made.

Maybe it was time to overcorrect the situation. She'd let herself get carried away with a fantasy that only had to exist outside this ranch house. Allison became used to sitting next to him on the couch in the evenings by the fire, but now she always chose a seat on the other side of the room. She tried not to look at him, but every time she did, she'd catch him looking at her. He'd quickly glance away, apparently as self-conscious as she'd been about their "almost" hook-up a week ago. Possibly also a bit embarrassed by how caught up they'd been in the moment.

Whenever his phone would buzz and he'd glance at it, then put it away without responding, she wondered if it was Perri again. She wondered if he'd already talked to her privately as he'd said he would. For all she knew, last week they were texting and making plans to get back together again when he returned to Seattle. Maybe he viewed that night as a wakeup call they were letting this fantasy get out of hand. They'd been close to making a choice from which there would be no coming back.

It would be so easy to fall into bed with Rowan, but it might also be a mistake.

Their friendship would not survive a casual fling. Last week, they'd allowed their hormones to rule the day and she could not have that happen again. Rowan always said the right things and she found that she believed him. But he was still very much on the rebound even if he didn't realize it. There was every possibility he'd come to regret a hookup with her. She didn't want him to have any misgivings when they went home to Seattle. She didn't want him left wondering whether he'd jumped too quickly into another relationship. He should not have any doubts. Hadn't he said that he tended to make bad decisions when it came to women?

She did not want to be one of those bad choices.

What if she'd been about to become another disappointment? A rash hookup best relegated to a vacation-style fling. Besides, their passion for each other didn't mean they had to rush into sleeping together. This relationship of theirs was a lot more than physical. She'd revealed so much to him, but not the most important thing: she'd fallen *in love* with him.

She had to talk to him, of course, and she could tell he wanted to talk, too. In the evenings, when they were all sitting around the fireplace with the family watching holiday shows, she'd catch him staring at her then quickly looking away. Privacy in the Abernathy household was not a thing and she'd been able to avoid a deep conversation.

Rowan, meanwhile, excelled at making the kids laugh. Often, she'd catch him playing video games with the boys. Jill always grabbed him whenever she wanted something too high to reach. Allison could tell Charlotte already adored him and Billy, too, was a fan.

Maybe later today, when she got back from the food drive, she'd find a private moment and explain why this couldn't happen. She'd list all the reasons why sleeping together would be a bad idea. He'd probably already decided the same thing and the conversation would be short.

After showering and dressing, Allison made it downstairs to find she wasn't the only one up. Jill was already dressed and eating from a box of sugary cereal.

"*That* doesn't look healthy. I'll make you a solid breakfast." Allison pulled out the cast-iron skillet.

"No worries, I don't have time. Mom's picking me and Nicky up in a few."

"What about the career fair? You're not doing it again this year?"

Last year, apparently Billy had dragged Jill to career day only to run into Charlotte, who'd been recruited to talk about careers in marine biology. And the rest was history.

As for Allison, she wasn't looking forward to revisiting old memories of the high school she'd just become used to when she'd been pulled out and hauled away to boarding school. She still remembered the expressions on her friends' faces when she'd announced she was leaving. But, funny thing, they'd all moved on fine without her. She couldn't fault them for that, but it had still stung to realize how easily she'd been forgotten.

"I did that last year. Maybe I'll drop in later. Depends on if Mom has anything special planned for us this weekend."

"What about Branson? What's he doing today?"

"Who knows?" Jill looked up with a conspiratorial smile. "Maybe hanging out with his girlfriend. Mom said he could meet us later."

Probably the same one he'd had for the past year. Allison hoped history wouldn't repeat itself.

"Oh! There she is!" Jill stood up, carrying her bowl of pink milk and depositing it in the sink. "Nicky! Mom's here!"

"See you la—" Allison called out.

The front door slammed shut. Two minutes later, the door opened and closed again. Looking out the kitchen window, she saw Nicky hop in the back seat of the dark luxury sedan and they all drove off.

"Good morning," Charlotte said. "Was that the kids taking off with Jane?"

Allison turned to her, spatula in hand. "Yes, and Nicky didn't even eat breakfast!"

"You are taking your role of breakfast dispenser seriously." Charlotte laughed. "She did come early, I got to admit."

"Well, I'll happily make a healthy breakfast for you. Have a seat and take a load off."

"Didn't you volunteer for the food drive? You better get going." Charlotte grabbed a mug from the cupboard. "Don't worry about me. I'll eat my overnight blueberry oats in the fridge."

"All right, if you're sure. But would you mind entertaining Rowan today?"

"Why don't you take him with you?"

"I thought I'd let him…you know, hang out at the ranch. Take a breather."

"You two haven't been anywhere in a week. What happened to letting everyone in town know you two are engaged?"

"I think we accomplished that perfectly." Allison held up her ring. "We actually may have…you know, overdone it."

"I know. You have a *ring.*"

"Safe to say pretty much everyone in Bronco believes we're engaged."

"It's no wonder. I half believe it myself."

That makes two of us.

This was dangerous because she wanted it all to be real and Rowan was doing his best to indulge her greatest fantasies about him. No wonder she'd been about to hop into bed with him.

"And, last week, after that performance…we almost…

we…" Allison spoke in a hushed tone. "Almost went up-stairs together."

Charlotte grinned. "Why didn't you?"

"Because it's not *real*." Allison crossed her arms.

"But you could change that. You want this to be real."

"I'm afraid to even say it out loud, but yes. I do."

"While I understand not wanting to hook up in a baby nursery with nosy teenagers in rooms on either side of you, I encourage you to go for it. At some point. You'd be a fool not to. I mean he's…you know…wow." Charlotte made a motion with her hands like that of a minor explosion.

"Who's wow?" a deep male voice said from the entrance to the kitchen.

Rowan. Oh dear. How much had he overheard? Allison felt her cheeks blaze with heat.

Charlotte's cheeks were as pinked as Allison's probably were. "Oh, the…um, the new high school biology teacher. One of the kids said something."

"Ah," Rowan said, grabbing a mug from the cupboard. "How's everyone this morning? What are the plans this weekend?"

"Well, Allison was just saying how she'd love to take you with her to the food drive," Charlotte said. "I know they always could use the extra help."

Allison shot her sister a warning look.

"Count me in," Rowan said. "You didn't mention it."

Allison brushed by him. "You've been busy and I didn't want to disturb you."

"I admit I got called into a Zoom meeting a couple of days ago but it turns out even grinches like me deserve a few days off around Christmas."

Grinches like him? What was he even talking about?

Rowan was like a hot Santa and an elf rolled up into one juicy male package.

"Okay, great. I'll just go get my jacket and gloves and meet you outside."

Chapter Fourteen

The sun shone brightly but Rowan felt the chill even inside Charlotte's SUV. Allison had mostly been avoiding him. He'd been waiting for the right moment to apologize for pushing too hard and too soon, but it had proved tough to catch her alone. A couple of times he'd thought of knocking on her door after bedtime, but he hadn't wanted to send the wrong message.

Hello, I'm here for a booty call.

Nope. Plus, both of their rooms were near nosy teenagers. So, it had been an entire week of dancing around each other, trying not to get into each other's space.

This was finally the moment he'd been waiting for and if it took an afternoon at the local high school, he didn't mind a bit.

"Hey, I'm sorry."

Allison started. "Why? What did you do?"

"I'm sorry if I put too much pressure on you. I got caught up in the moment and scared you off."

She snorted. "You didn't scare me. I scared myself. All these feelings I have. They're so intense and I'm confused."

"And then I came in guns blazing. My fault."

"I wanted to be with you that night, and without the kids' interruption, it would have happened."

"But…?" He sensed her thought wasn't complete.

"Maybe that would have been a mistake." She gripped the steering wheel. "Our friendship is too precious to me, and we wouldn't survive a fling."

"Good, because I don't want a fling."

But he cursed his lousy timing since he didn't want to wait an appropriate amount of time before he could seriously date Allison. What was the arbitrary number of days a man should wait before he went after the woman he'd wanted to be with all along? The thought of dating someone else, anyone else, did not even slightly appeal to him. He didn't want to waste any time when he already knew who he wanted. When he already understood who would be perfect for him, and he for her.

"We're agreed then. No fling."

"Absolutely *not*." He waited a beat. "I mean we're engaged. Would we even qualify as a fling?" Yeah, that was a reach on his part, and he had to force his lips to keep from quirking into a smile.

Allison gave him a sideways smirk. "Nice try."

After a few minutes, Allison pulled into a parking space at the high school near the auditorium entrance and, together, they followed the signs pointing toward the food drive. The building looked like an ordinary secondary school with well-manicured lawns and the appropriate school spirit signs stating, "Go Mustangs!"

"So, this is where you went to high school."

"For about a year, until my parents shipped me off to boarding school."

It hadn't occurred to him how difficult this might be for Allison. He mostly had fond memories of his high school days, but he'd excelled at football. If not for that, he might have hated every second of those insecure years. One of his best friends had been mercilessly teased for his acne-pockmarked face and Rowan had appointed himself his personal bodyguard. High school could be hell for some kids and with social media, he'd heard it was even worse now.

"What was that year like for you?"

"Good if not perfect, because you know…high school. I went with some of my best friends. Kids I'd grown up with all through grade school. I was the kind of student filled with school spirit. Tried out for the cheerleading team and made it for my sophomore year. Unfortunately, I never even had a chance to order the uniform."

Rowan reached for Allison's hand and squeezed it. The hint of regret in her words pierced him in the heart. *Ouch.*

"Well, honestly, you probably didn't miss much."

He was lying. She'd missed going to high school with the friends she'd known her entire life. All those connections and relationships. She'd been torn out of the world she'd loved and understood.

"Right. High school is just four years of a kid's life. College was better and, bonus, I was already accustomed to being away from home. I could have taught the graduate course."

Somehow, that didn't make him feel any better. He continued to hold her hand, only letting go to swing open the double doors. There were more signs pointing one way to the career fair and in the other direction for the food drive. He followed Allison, hanging behind, giving her space.

By a large sign indicating they'd reached the food drive, conveniently across from the cafeteria, a group of people had gathered around lunch tables and cardboard boxes. The student body president introduced herself.

"We've already got barrels and barrels of nonperishable food and more coming in all day," she said. "I'm pairing all the couples up, so you two can come over this way and start putting family boxes together. One of each item. Later on, we're going to be making the deliveries so everyone can have a Christmas dinner."

Working with Allison was easy, because as he'd already noticed they seemed to be in tune with each other. It was as if he could anticipate her next move and she could do the same for him. As activity buzzed all around them, the students accepted donations then placed them in one area. One couple was making up the boxes and two other couples were helping to put together the boxes. Two gravy packets, a box of premade stuffing, canned green beans, and all the typical items.

While other couples were bumping into each other, at times putting in the same items, he and Allison had a system. There was a reason they were friends. They had a natural cohesiveness. A way they simply fit together.

They'd been working in sync for an hour when a teacher ran up to Allison.

"One of our presenters had car trouble and isn't going to make it to career day. Do you think I could pull you away from here to present? Could you talk about careers in IT?"

Allison blinked. "Sorry."

"Oh, you're from Seattle, so I just assumed."

"A common assumption," Allison deadpanned.

"I don't know what I'm going to do! I have a classroom full of teenagers and if I don't provide a speaker, there's no telling what will happen."

Rowan lightly touched the younger woman's shoulder. "I can talk about careers in IT."

She whipped her head around. "Who are you? Do I know you?"

"This is my fiancé, Rowan Scott."

"Oh, you're from Seattle, too?"

"I am." Rowan nodded. "I've worked in IT since I graduated from college. I've been employed by Microsoft and others."

"Rowan," Allison interrupted, "they've put you on the spot, and that's not fair."

"But it would really help. Just sayin'." The teacher tossed her hair and swiped through her tablet.

Allison took his hand and pulled him aside. "Listen, you don't have to do this. It's *my* old high school and if anyone should be obligated, it's me."

"But what will they do with a classroom full of students and no speaker?"

"Well, that's not your problem, is it?"

"Don't look now, but you sound like the Grinch." He tapped her chin.

"I would do it, honestly, but—"

Ah, she felt guilty about not doing this herself and throwing him to the wolves. But this was his wheelhouse.

"Yeah, I know. You prefer to be better prepared, and I understand that. But here's one thing you don't know about me: I'm gifted with the rare ability to actually enjoy public speaking."

Allison gasped. "You're a unicorn."

"A professor once taught me the secret of a twenty-minute speech on any given subject. You want to hear it?"

"Of course."

"First, you start with an acronym regarding your subject. Shorter words are for shorter speeches. For this talk, I'll probably use TECHNOLOGY. Starting with the letter T, I'll mention a few basics about technology. Then I'll move on to the letter E, possibly educational requirements. With C, I'll go to careers in tech. And so on, letter by letter. No matter the subject, it's an easy way to do a last-minute speech."

"Great way to organize the talk in your head. I'll have to remember that. Unlike you, I'm not a huge fan of public speaking. I'm okay in small groups."

The teacher rejoined them. "I'm sorry, but if you're doing this, I need to know. Otherwise, I have to go run and ask every adult here today and I better get going. Please?"

Rowan held out his arm. "Just lead the way."

"Thank you!"

He squeezed Allison's hand one last time and followed the teacher down the hallways into a classroom filled with students.

"Allison!"

When she turned a few minutes later, Allison recognized her friend and former classmate, Zuri.

"Hey, how are you?"

A strange feeling had gripped Allison as she'd walked down the old hallways and wound up straight across from the cafeteria where, for an entire year, she'd sat to eat lunch and gossip with friends. She hadn't expected to see any of those friends here today. Zuri looked almost exactly like Allison remembered her, with black corkscrew curls and flawless latte skin.

"I'm great, but not as good as you!" She turned in the direction Rowan had walked. "Who was *that* with you?"

Allison wasn't going to lie. It gave her great satisfaction to say, "That's my fiancé, Rowan Scott."

Zuri waved her hand in a "too hot to handle" motion. "Girl! Congratulations."

"Thanks."

Zuri had been the one in high school with so many interested boys chasing after her that Allison lost count. She remembered how envious she'd been of Zuri's easy popularity but also incredibly grateful of how kind and generous she'd been. A year older than Allison, she'd suggested Allison try out for the cheerleading squad. Zuri had sensed Allison's insecurities and encouraged her to "wear the coat." When Allison asked what she meant, she'd borrowed her jacket, shrugged it on and strutted back and forth. Allison's plain sheepskin suddenly looked like the sharp coat of a movie star on the red carpet when Zuri wore it. And she swore it wasn't the jacket. It was the way she *wore* it.

"How've you been?"

"I'm a new teacher here. I just started teaching biology."

Allison bit her lower lip. So, this was the "wow" teacher Charlotte had mentioned. Funny, she'd pictured a man, and definitely not one of her old high school chums.

"That's you? I've already heard all kinds of good things about the new biology teacher. Billy's kids are apparently impressed."

"It's been a whirlwind." She smiled and cocked her head. "Hey, you look fantastic. I always wondered what happened to you after high school."

Allison wondered if everyone in town had come to their own conclusions. Personally, she'd never bothered to ask. Charlotte had moved on, and Allison tried to be equally as resilient, even if it hadn't been her choice to leave Bronco.

"After college, I wasn't sure what I wanted to do with my liberal arts degree, so I followed my sister Charlotte to Seattle. When she wound up leaving to do her marine biology thing in the Bahamas, I stayed. I love living in the city and I have a nice career there in human resources."

"Well, it's so good to see you," Zuri said, turning in the

direction of an approaching student. "And we'll catch up some more at the cookie exchange."

"Cookie exchange?"

And in the next moment, Allison groaned when she remembered. When she'd first arrived in Bronco, Eloise had invited her to a cookie exchange on Christmas Eve. There'd been so much going on since Rowan arrived that she hadn't spoken to Eloise recently and the whole event had slipped her mind.

"At your sister Eloise's."

"Right, I remember now."

"You've been busy, I take it, with your dreamboat fiancé." She winked.

"Yes, uh-huh, but I'll—we'll—be there." Allison gave her old friend a smile.

"See you then." Zuri waved and walked away, curls bouncing. No less than four students and two adult volunteers followed her with their eyes as she *strutted* off.

A few minutes later, unable to resist the temptation any longer, Allison excused herself from the food drive. Trying her hand at "wearing the coat" she strut-walked toward the classrooms, following the Career Fair signs. While she thought it might be difficult to find the exact classroom, all she had to do was peek inside an open door with standing room only.

Rowan stood at the front of the class, commanding the room. Though she'd always found him attractive, and even if she'd already realized something very real was happening between them, now something unnamed slid into place. And, like a key finding its lock, it clicked. She found nothing quite as alluring as watching a man thrive in his element. Whether it was on the range, in the boardroom or in a classroom.

She listened, spellbound, for the next several minutes as Rowan spoke effortlessly and after a while took questions from the students. He was dressed simply in jeans and a flannel shirt but might as well be wearing a pin-striped, tailor-made suit. Someone had once showed Rowan had to "wear the coat," or it simply came naturally to him. He oozed self-confidence and, seriously, was there anything more attractive than a self-assured and intelligent man?

When he was done speaking, he received a standing ovation. And Allison even noticed a number of students gazing, dreamy-eyed, at Rowan.

Get in line, kids.

Chapter Fifteen

After the career fair, Allison took Rowan to lunch to thank him. He'd come through for the students, and people were already talking about how Allison Taylor's "fiancé from Seattle" saved the day. They wound up at Bronco Burgers again, site of the place where afterward they'd gone home and almost slept together. After a juicy burger and fries, Allison was ready to tackle the rest of the day.

Last night, Jill had begged for help wrapping her presents, since she'd be gone all this weekend with her mother. The boys wanted help, too, claiming to be "all thumbs," even if Branson was practically an expert roper. He wasn't fooling her. She guessed she and Rowan would be wrapping their presents for the next two days. Nothing like leaving it till the last minute.

On the drive home, she caught him up on the talk she'd had with Zuri.

"I was reminded there's a cookie exchange at my sister Eloise's place on Christmas Eve. There will be plenty of people there, some that might know my parents. So, I'll have to call on you once more to play the part of devoted fiancé."

"Great. I was wondering when I would have a chance to reprise my award-winning performance." Rowan winked.

"Eloise had a baby last December, but at least Charlotte's baby will be born well after the holidays. It's a tough time to have a birthday."

"Are you going to stay in Montana until after Charlotte's baby is born?"

"That was the plan."

"Then I guess I won't see you for another month once I go back."

"Yes."

A silence settled between them.

By the time she got home, he and Perri might already be reunited, leaving any opportunity for the two of them gone. Oh, he'd be kind and give Allison a gentle brush-off because he'd want to stay friends and good neighbors. But despite the fact she'd tried to reign in her feelings, Allison would be heartbroken.

"By the way, you don't really have to stay until New Year's Eve. I think we only told that *particular* lie to Frederick, and we can always make up some excuse as to why you had to go home early."

Rowan stayed quiet, his gaze on the beautiful Montana wintry day outside.

The forecast called for snow in the next few days and, with any luck, a white Christmas.

"Is it okay with you if I stay?"

She was a bit taken aback by the words, which sounded almost wistful.

"You're enjoying Montana that much?"

"I guess I'd have to say that I'm enjoying hanging out with *you*. The location doesn't really matter."

She was glad to be driving, so she could avoid meeting his eyes. Because she knew that in hers, he'd be able to see all the longing for him she'd been trying to tamp down.

Raw emotion stirred through her. "Me, too. I'm never going to forget this time. Promise me something. No matter what happens when you get back, we'll always be friends."

"I promise."

It felt like her heart hung on the edge of a precipice, waiting for a shove into the abyss.

She had wanted to avoid heartache, but it was too late now.

On Christmas Eve as planned, they headed to the Heights Hotel in Bronco Heights for Eloise's cookie exchange.

Rowan, for his part, seemed ecstatic about the thought of more cookies.

"Honestly, we had two days to bake the cookies. Why didn't we?" Rowan said.

"Are you forgetting the presents we've been wrapping nonstop?"

There had been no time to bake. She'd fed the family no-frills lunches and dinners, and a couple of times Rowan had run out for more of that pizza.

The guilty plastic-wrapped plate of store-bought cookies sat in her lap as Rowan drove them to the cookie exchange. She could have carried the cookies in the cute pink box from the store, but they were trying to pass them off as their own.

"Don't worry." Rowan squeezed her leg now. "Our cookie secret is safe. No one will ever know the difference."

Earlier today, while Allison had been helping Charlotte sort, fold and stack baby clothes in the nursery, he'd driven into town to place an order of snickerdoodles and gingerbread men. They'd planned to pass them off as their own, and considering this was a gathering with more than just Eloise and Dante, they would continue the engagement ruse, too.

"Let's leave as soon as we can," Allison said. "I still have a few presents to wrap before tomorrow morning and I don't want to stay up too late."

"Mine?" he said.

"What makes you think I got you anything?" she teased.

"Your reaction on the day we went shopping, when I offered to bring in your packages. You said, and I quote, 'Keep your paws off my shopping bags, Scott!' I'd like to think you wouldn't say that if you weren't hiding something from me."

"Okay, maybe I did get you something." She smiled and shifted in her seat. "And you never told me. Is your mother terribly unhappy about you spending Christmas away from home?"

"No," Rowan said simply. "She's absolutely fine with it. I said I'd make it up to her next year. I also discovered something fairly surprising. Apparently, Grayson's fiancée is stressed about hosting at their home this year. She will have one less thing to worry about without me there."

"What does that mean? Do you have any food allergies I'm not aware of?"

He shrugged. "Apparently, they both try hard to impress me, which is ironic."

"Is it though?" She laughed, realizing once more how differently people saw themselves. "You don't seem to realize how much people rely on you. At our complex, whenever something is broken or not working, we all ask you. That time the WiFi was out, remember? It was as if you could magically fix it for all of us."

He shrugged. "Everyone thinks when you're in tech that you know more than you actually do."

"You know a lot more than you want to admit. And you help everyone who asks, so it's no wonder people appreciate you. Let's start with you helping me move in because my lame boyfriend didn't show up until later."

"I wasn't raised to stand by and watch a woman carry a TV upstairs. I let you take the little stuff, didn't I?"

"Yes, you did. How kind of you."

He was a born helper and had grown up in the shadow of a flashier brother. And she'd been stuck in old patterns, thinking that her father still had some control over her when he didn't. He hadn't controlled her for years. Even though she worked hard to keep the family peace, it was more for her mother's sake. Hence the lie about being engaged so she didn't have to be rude and tell her father to go jump off a bridge.

"Tell me more about your sister Eloise."

"She's the youngest in our family, and yet the first to have a baby. You'll meet her little girl Merry, who's a year old now. Even though I'm closest in age to Charlotte, I guess you could say Eloise and I bonded over the fact that in a way we were both punished for Charlotte's mistake."

"She went to boarding school, too?"

"Yes, and she also didn't come back to Bronco for many years. She lived in New York City and had a highly successful marketing business. The funny thing is, even as a grown woman, she still had a baby before being married."

"Bet good old Thaddeus wasn't too jazzed about that."

"Lighting striking twice? Not at all. But once the baby was born, all was forgiven. Merry's their first grandchild, and quite adorable. I didn't get to hang out with her much last year, so I'm excited to see her today."

They parked in the hotel's visitor parking area and took the elevator to the fifth floor. Allison knocked and the door swung open to Eloise, wearing a red-and-white sweater exactly like Allison's.

"Hey, great taste in sweaters." Allison pointed.

"We're twinning!" Eloise took the cookie plate from Allison and led them both inside the hotel suite. She leaned in to whisper, "Hey, and great taste in men."

"Eloise, this is Rowan Scott, my...my fiancé." Allison made the introductions for the others in the room to hear. "He came out from Seattle to help me with Charlotte and her family."

"And, I heard from Charlotte, to run interference with our blowhard of a father," Eloise said in a hushed tone. "Don't worry, your secret is safe with me."

"I'm surprised to find you all still at the hotel," Allison said. "Why aren't you in the house yet?"

Eloise and her husband Dante started renovating the fixer-upper they'd bought nearly a year ago. She'd sent Allison photos via text of the modest, three bedroom house with a basketball hoop in the driveway. If it were Allison, with a one-year-old, she'd be more than ready to give up hotel life.

"Everything took far longer than we expected. I'm sick of contractors. But it should be ready to move into any day now. Probably right before Dante goes back to school after the holiday break. We've already moved some of our stuff, and it's sitting in boxes in the finished garage."

"Where's my adorable niece?" Allison said. "Must get my baby fix."

"Fair warning, Merry has the sniffles and we've been mostly staying in. I don't want to take her around Charlotte, either, since she's so close to her due date."

Eloise and Dante's apartment was decorated with a Douglas Fir, dozens of brightly colored wrapped presents under it. Allison always felt that Christmas was mostly for young children.

It must be wonderful to have your own little family, she mused, wondering how many of those presents under the tree were for Merry.

Dante came over, holding the baby. She wore a dress similar to the one Allison had picked out at Hey, Baby: a frilly green-and-white dress with a matching hairband. She was still mostly bald, only a few blond hairs sticking up, and she was adorable.

Dante must have sensed her baby fever, so he handed Merry over. She didn't cry or scream but simply checked Allison out like she was a new, bright and shiny object.

Allison hadn't expected tears to well in her eyes, but they did. As if he sensed it, somehow, Rowan was right behind her, one hand steady on her lower back. She had come to rely on his solid presence.

"Hi, Merry," Allison said. "I'm your Aunt Allison. I'll be the one sending you US savings bonds over the years. It will be tough, but just wait until they mature."

Dante chuckled. He probably appreciated that low-key financial lesson for his daughter.

"Goo," Merry said, and stretched her chubby little arms out for her mother.

Eloise took the baby back, far too soon for Allison, but she wasn't there for a baby fix. She was there to make an appearance and bring a big tray of cookies back to the Abernathy house, following which, the children would nominate her for sainthood.

After Dante introduced a few of his colleagues from the local school where he worked as a third-grade teacher, they were led into the suite's small but modern kitchen where the tiny gray-granite countertop was filled with plates of cookies. Eloise put their offering with the rest.

The event turned out to be like an open house. Friends

were coming and going for hours. Zuri eventually arrived with a tall, well-dressed and really gorgeous man by her side.

"Hey, good to see you." She hugged Allison. "Please meet my date, Marcus."

"Hi, Marcus." Allison settled her hand on Rowan's chest. "This is my fiancé, Rowan Scott."

"Please to meet you both." Rowan offered his hand, but Zuri circumvented and grabbed a hug instead.

Smart girl.

"You're the one who saved the day at the career fair," she said.

"Ah, it was nothing. My pleasure."

After a while, Allison noticed people loading up on cookies. A few from each of the trays, making a potpourri of scrumptious Christmas confections.

Allison moved to the counters, in awe at the many choices. "And to think I've never been to a cookie exchange before."

"The Sanchez family does this every year and so we figured we'd start our own tradition," Eloise piped up.

"Any word on Winona?" Allison asked. The thought of poor Stanley, alone at this time of the year and missing his fiancée was disheartening.

"No," Eloise said. "The Sanchez family is just trying to get through the holidays. It's tough."

"I can only imagine," Rowan said. "Just the thought of Allison taking off on me on our wedding day makes me sick. It would break my heart. I have no idea what I'd do."

There was such sincerity in his voice, Allison wanted to believe desperately that this wasn't an act. Rowan took the lead and started loading up their plate with a few of each cookie. There were chocolate-chip cookies, butter cookies, Russian teacakes, caramel sea salt cookies, brownies, almond biscotti, and lemon cookies.

"Sampling is allowed," Eloise chuckled.

She didn't have to tell Allison twice. After some sampling, she decided the lemon cookies were her favorite. By the time they were done, the plate was about three levels high.

"This ought to keep the Abernathy kids happy," Allison said.

"What? These cookies are for you," Eloise said. "Take another plate for the kids."

Allison and Rowan exchanged a look.

"If you insist."

Sampling did take place, but in the end, the gathering seemed to be more of a cocktail party than a cookie exchange. Most everyone imbibed from the spiked punch and one of the teachers took orders at a makeshift bar.

"Can I make you a drink?" she said. "Just name it. Anything! I bartended my way all through college."

"How about a Cosmo?" Allison said.

She pointed. "You're trying to trip me up, but I know how to make it! Just give me a second."

Allison finished the drink and, damn, if everybody here didn't suddenly look extremely pretty. But she'd always been a lightweight. She noted Rowan had been whisked away by a few females who now seemed to be hanging on his every word. She'd lay money down that Rowan had not noticed the women were licking their lips and tossing their hair for his benefit. But Allison had. It made her a little sick to her stomach. If she didn't step up her game, she was going to lose Rowan. Not tonight, but soon, to someone who had the nerve to tell him how she felt. To someone willing to tell him she loved him and wanted a future with him.

She joined Rowan just in time for someone to ask about his fiancée.

"Here she is." He put an arm around Allison, drawing her close. "The one I was telling you about."

"You were talking about me?" Allison said. "I'm sorry I missed this."

"He was just telling us how you met," one of the women said. "Adorable meet cute."

"So, what are you guys going to do now that you're engaged? Keep one apartment or move into a house together?" another woman asked.

The question stumped her as much as it did Rowan. Real estate prices in Seattle were astronomical. She hadn't thought about any of this.

"Well... I think we will probably move into one apartment and save for the wedding," Rowan said.

"Yeah, that makes sense," Allison said. "I like my apartment."

Rowan squeezed her shoulder. He probably liked his apartment, too. She couldn't be so set in her ways not to at least consider his apartment. It was slightly bigger than hers but didn't have a view. Oh wait. This wasn't even happening. It didn't matter because they weren't engaged. Right.

The truth was he'd go back to Seattle first and maybe this time around when he reconciled with Perri, she would actually move in with him.

"Would you ever move back to Bronco?" someone else asked.

"I don't think so," Allison said, even while she realized she would miss seeing Merry grow up. She'd miss watching Charlotte and Billy's baby grow up, too.

"But we will come back to visit often," Rowan said.

"I would like that," Allison said. "The truth is, Rowan can work from anywhere."

"Definitely a perk."

Allison turned to see Eloise beckoning her, so she excused herself and followed her sister to her bedroom.

"What's up?" Allison said.

"I thought we could talk privately in here."

"About what?"

"For starters...um, tell me about this ring!" Eloise reached for Allison's ring finger and held it up to inspect. "It's gorgeous. Where did you get it?"

"Rowan gave it to me. We were shopping at Sadie's Holiday House and he thought it would be a good idea for me to have a ring. If we were really going to sell this engagement thing to the town."

She thought of how he'd given it to her and then lifted her up and spun her around to "make it look good." Even now, the memory made her heart tug with a powerful emotion. What had been the game they intended it to be was still real to him, but her feelings were real.

"That seems over the top for a game you two are playing."

"I'm not sure it's a game anymore. At least, not for me."

"How long have you been crushing on this man? Isn't this the guy you told me was simply your neighbor?"

Allison opened her mouth to object but there was hardly a point anymore. She was, apparently, obvious to the people who knew her well.

"It's been a while that I've been having stronger feelings for him, but, honestly, we were just friends."

"*Were* being the operative word."

"I don't know what's going to happen. We'll just have to see when we get back to Seattle. He's going to go home before I do, and I think that's when he and his ex will reconcile. She still wants him and who can blame her."

"He seems really into you. And the ring just proves it. He didn't have to do that, I'm sure you know."

"Yes, we could have just said the ring was being sized. I guess he wanted to. Honestly, I'm…a little crazy about him."

"I can see that. Have you told him?"

"We've been very…affectionate, even in private when we don't need to pretend."

"'Fake it 'til you make it' takes on a whole new meaning." Eloise smiled then sobered as Allison didn't share the humor. "Why do I sense a hesitation from you?"

"Because he's too good to be true? Mostly, because he's just off a breakup with a woman he dated for two years."

"Great. So, he's not a commitment-phobe. He really hangs in there."

Leave it to Eloise to spin this in a positive light.

"Yes, true, but he might also not be completely over his ex. And, more to the point, I doubt she's going to leave him alone. She's been texting him almost the whole time he's been in Bronco."

Eloise groaned. "Not good. You're worried they're not really done with each other. But what does he say? You have asked him."

It wasn't a question. Allison would have been silly not to bring it up.

"He says it's over, but he's said that before. Their pattern involves going back and forth with each other. I just don't want to be a casualty in their on-again, off-again dysfunction."

"You might not be. If they're not right for each other, and you can see it, just give it some time. He'll come to the same conclusion when he can compare his old relationship to a high-functioning one. Be patient."

Allison wanted to be patient. She wanted to believe with

all her heart things would work out this time. But for her, the things she desperately wanted usually did not work out.

"You know what? For a little sister, you give great advice."

Chapter Sixteen

Allison left the girl-talk moment with Eloise reassured. No matter what happened, Rowan would have this time they'd had together to measure against any possible future he may or may not have with Perri. Even though they'd broken up before, maybe this time was different. He'd said so, for one thing. She should take him at his word. And, more to the point, she didn't think Rowan had ever dated anyone else between breakups, definitely not seriously. Plus, there was the fact he'd been attracted to her from the start of their relationship and simply not acted on his feelings. Add the additional fact that they'd never both been free and single at the same time before now.

When she and Eloise rejoined the others in the living room, Allison caught a sight that took her breath away.

"Oh. My." She brought a hand to her chest.

Rowan sat on the couch, Merry in his lap. She was turned to him, her little chubby, and likely sticky, fingers reaching for his chin. Just the way he held her, so gently and tenderly, while at the same time seeming completely enthralled with her, sent a strong jolt of awareness through Allison. He'd been so good with the Abernathy kids all this time, too, joking around with Nicky and Branson. More than once, they'd asked for his advice on a video game world they were both trying to conquer. Apparently, Rowan had long ago reached the highest level, so he'd become a demigod to them.

And the day after the first snow, she had caught him in the front yard with Jill, helping her build a snowman. It must have been freezing, and he didn't exactly own a winter wardrobe, but that hadn't stopped him when she'd asked him to help her.

He would be a good father. No. An amazing father.

Allison came to sit beside him. "Hey."

He turned to her, grinning. "I think she likes me. She hasn't spit up on me or screamed once."

"Well, don't jinx it." Allison smiled and tugged gently on Merry's shiny patent-leather shoe.

Just sitting here, next to him, she pretended for a little slice of time. For this moment, and only this moment, Merry was their daughter. Rowan was her husband. She told herself it wasn't any different than pretending she was engaged to this man, but somehow this felt much more intimate. Real. She and Rowan fit together, and she couldn't deny any longer that she wanted this. *All* of this. A family, but not just any family.

A family with him.

The thought scared her since it came ripe with possible heartache, but for the first time in her life, there was less a sense of fear than excitement that filled her. She had to stop thinking of all the ways this could go wrong, and start imagining all the ways this could go right.

On the way home, it began to snow again. Allison had to admit the soft white flakes cast the town in an almost ethereal glow.

"Something about the snow makes me feel like it's truly Christmas," she said. "My sisters and I used to pray every

year for a white Christmas. Then again, we were spared
the shoveling."

"My brother and I also had a tradition. We used to sleep
by the fireplace hoping we'd catch Santa in the act. I had a
notepad nearby so I could keep track of clues left behind."

"Aw, how sweet." Just the memory of a young Rowan
made her heart squeeze.

"So, tell me. What's your favorite Christmas movie?"
Rowan asked.

"That's a tough one. I love all the Hallmark holiday mov-
ies, but my ageless favorite classic is *It's a Wonderful Life*."

"Good choice, sweetheart," Rowan said in a pretty amazing imitation of the classic Jimmy Stewart drawl. "Why,
you've got good taste. Shall I lasso the moon for you?"

"That's not bad." Allison laughed. "And what's your favorite Christmas movie?"

"Die Hard," they both said at once.

Allison laughed again. "Okay, tough guy, somehow I
knew that was your answer. I'll allow it."

"Sorry, but your favorite classic makes me cry."

She narrowed her eyes. "Really?"

"A tear came down my cheek one time when my mother
insisted we all watch it as a family."

"A *single* tear."

"What? That's considered *crying*."

She nudged his elbow. "And what about favorite Christmas song?"

"Definitely 'I Saw Mommy Kissing Santa Claus.' There's
something about knowing mom and dad are still getting it
on that's enormously appealing to me."

"That makes sense. I agree." Allison cleared her throat.
"But I'd have to say my favorite is 'Silent Night.' Charlotte

and Billy are fans of *The Nutcracker*, and I do like Tchai-kovsky."

They were halfway home when the snow really started to come down.

"Are you sure you can handle this?" Allison asked. "Maybe I should drive."

He squinted, his eyes never leaving the road. "Should I be offended? You know, I've definitely driven in the snow before. Maybe you forget it snows in Washington, too."

"But not like this. I think we'll have at least three inches by morning."

"Hey, maybe we'll get snowed in." The thought seemed to cheer him.

She hoped so, because the idea of having an excuse not to go to her parents' big holiday party and instead stay home in front of a fire, cuddling with Rowan, held enormous appeal.

"You *want* to get snowed in?"

"With you, the idea has appeal."

He never seemed to give up on finding a moment with her, even if it seemed unlikely with the lack of privacy. She'd started to give up on the idea, thinking it best not to take that risk with her heart. If he was serious about ending things with Perri, it would become evident once he went home and might run into her again.

"Um, about that…" she said. "I'm sorry we haven't found much privacy. I do want to be alone with you. You know that, right?"

"I'd hoped so, but it's good to hear it out loud."

"The moment hasn't been right."

She saw him nod in the light of the dash.

"My friends who are married say that's what happens when the kids become teenagers," he said. "It's back to when they were two, but worse, because they have a key to the house and the car. So, it's no surprise with a household of teens that there's little privacy for anyone."

"But we'll have all the privacy we want when we go home."

It was the first time she'd spoken her thoughts out loud. When they went home, she wanted to continue where'd they left off. If that's what he wanted, too. She waited to hear him agree and the silence seemed to stretch between them. She'd expressed clearly that this was what she wanted.

He was what she wanted.

"Is…is that what you want, too?" she asked him finally.

His head jerked in surprise. "Are you kidding? I thought I made myself pretty clear. I'm crazy about you."

Hearing the words said out loud was like someone had inflated her chest like a balloon. She was…full. It was like getting what she'd always wanted for Christmas. The best, most impossible gift.

"I really like you, Rowan. I always have. But you've been…" She didn't even want to say her name. "Dating someone for the past two years."

"Not anymore," he said. "I keep telling you—that's over."

He'd said that before, and she didn't want to argue with him anymore. Maybe it *would* be different this time. She hoped.

"But I understand how you must feel. Let's just…take it slow." He skimmed his warm hands down her arms.

"That's…that's a good idea." She framed his face, mesmerized by his gorgeous mouth.

"Here's the thing… If I'm being honest, I was checking you out the day I helped you move into the building. And then your boyfriend at the time showed up. So, this isn't really new. Not for me."

She sighed. "It's not new for me either."

The snow was still falling when they pulled up to Billy and Charlotte's house. It looked cold enough to be an unpleasant walk the few yards to the main house. She reluctantly unhooked her seat belt and went for the car door, but Rowan stilled her hand.

"Hang on."

"It's okay. I'll make a run for it. We'll thaw in front of the fireplace."

"I have an idea." He threaded her fingers through hers. "This, right here, is a private space."

"You have a point." She glanced outside. "It's also quite warm in here, at least for now."

"And we'll make it hot."

She slid across the bench seat until she was so close she could smell his delightful scent. He smelled like sandalwood and one hundred percent Rowan. Her hands went against his strong, firm chest. She wanted to see him naked. Wanted to see him at least without his shirt.

"Hey, stranger," he said, brushing a kiss across her knuckles. "Have I ever told you how much you intrigue me?"

She traced along his jawline. "Me?"

Of all the sisters, she may have been the least interesting. She'd followed Charlotte to Seattle after college, when her older sister moved. After she'd had to move for her marine biology work, Allison stayed in the city. She couldn't picture herself living in the Bahamas where Charlotte had relocated. While her job in human resources didn't exactly make Allison an adrenaline junkie, she liked her work just fine. Every once in a while, there was a bit of employee drama or juicy gossip that proved to be just enough for her. She'd had a childhood filled with drama and she hadn't wanted any more of it. So, *interesting* was never a word associated with herself.

"Yeah, you're intriguing," he said. "Because you come from such wealth, but you're such a simple girl. So down to earth. And gorgeous. You really slay me with your smile."

How nice for him to mention her smile. Not her legs or her behind, which most men seemed to zero in on. Rowan liked her *smile*.

The strong beat of his heart thumped under the pads of her fingers as she pressed her mouth to his. He kissed her with purpose, as if she was the most precious thing he'd ever touched. His tough beard stubble scraped against her sensitive flesh as he kissed down the column of her neck. She moaned, fisting his shirt, practically climbing into his lap. This wasn't going to work. She wanted more of him. More than she would get in the cab of this truck.

"You make me feel like a teenager with his first crush," Rowan said, his talented fingers roaming under her sweater, making her tingle and squirm for more.

"I wish we'd met a long time ago. I've wanted someone like you. I've looked for someone like you."

This was the time to tell him. *Tell him. Tell him.*

Tell him you love him.

But the words felt too big. Life-changing. She'd never say those words to him without knowing the impact they might have. Good or bad. She could scare him away, or she might get everything she'd ever wanted.

"This is going so fast," she said, breathless.

"Too fast for you?" he whispered, his warm breath fanning against her neck.

"Too fast and yet not fast enough."

She kissed him again, threading her fingers through his thick hair, tugging him close. And it wasn't close enough. Out of the corner of her eye, she noticed they were fogging up the windows. "I think we need something to cool us down." Allison laughed.

"You might be correct. Much more of this and I'll be tearing off your clothes."

"Or tearing off *your* clothes." She smirked. "I have an idea." She swung open her door. "Come with me."

"Where are we going now?"

She reached for his hand and tugged him along the freshly fallen snow to the perfect spot.

"I haven't done this since I was a kid."

Then she dropped to her back and lay down in the powdery snow.

"Allison? What are you—"

The moment after she began to flail her arms and legs in half circles, he dropped down a couple feet next to her to do the same.

"Snow angels," he said. "Yeah, I remember this."

Delight pulsed through Allison and she didn't care she was cold and would soon also be wet. Memories came back of some of the best days she'd spent in Bronco as a child with her sisters and brothers. The first snow of the season meant running outside to catch snowflakes on her tongue, making a snowman, sledding down the hill in the back of their property, and snow angels.

Those were the better days, before she'd ever disappointed her parents enough to be sent away from home.

She got a kick out of watching Rowan beside her, laughing and smiling with her. The last boyfriend she'd had would have never wanted to mess up his precious hair enough to cut loose like this. He would have called her a nutcase. But Rowan was so playful right along with her, so fun and open to just about anything.

Allison stood to admire her snow angel on the ground, and so did Rowan.

"Yours is bigger," she said.

"But yours is better." He took two steps toward her and took her hand. "Now that we're both cold and damp, I have to tell you something."

"Yeah? What's that?" She wiped a damp strand of hair from her face.

"This isn't working." He gave her as slow smile, which moved from his crinkly eyes to eventually take over his whole face. "I'm still picturing you naked."

"Same. And I have to say, you look fantastic."

He laughed, a deep and hearty sound, took her hand and led her back to the truck to get the plate of cookies.

"We can't forget these."

"Absolutely not. That's my ticket into sainthood with the kids." She took the plate of cookies from him and hugged them to her chest.

"Just please make sure I get one of those snickerdoodles." Rowan steered her inside, hand low on her back. "Whomever baked those is the one who should be canonized."

"Rowan, you can have all the snickerdoodles."

"Score," he said, and then gave her a sweet kiss.

And later that night after prep time for the morning breakfast and another warm kiss in the hallway with Rowan, Allison barely slept. It was a bit like being a little girl again, anticipation thrumming through her on what she might find under the tree in the morning. Whether or not Santa had listened and brought what she'd asked for.

This time, the dreams and hopes were bigger. They were wishes for a future with the man of her dreams. He was only two doors down from her right now, not all that differently than he had been for the past few years when he'd simply been her neighbor across the hall. Handsome, smart and funny. Unavailable.

But now, possibilities shimmered like stars in an evening sky.

Chapter Seventeen

On Christmas morning, Allison woke with a deep sense of happiness and excitement such as she hadn't experienced since being a small child. She'd always loved Christmas Day when she and her siblings would wake before sunrise. Their parents would force them to stay in their bedrooms until the sun came up, but after that, it was fair game. As they grew into teenagers there was less excitement early in the morning, everyone sleeping in. Allison expected this would be the case in the Abernathy household. But in a few years, there would be a little one ready to rush downstairs and find what Santa brought.

Before anyone else woke, Allison showered and dressed, planning to start a big breakfast for the family. She'd peeled potatoes and mixed pancake batter the night before. It would be a down-home, big-country breakfast, the way her mother's cook used to make.

It's a Wonderful Life played softly on the TV screen in the background while Allison brewed coffee and cooked. She couldn't wait to see how everyone liked their gifts. A great deal of thought had gone into each one.

As she bent to put a tray of biscuits in the oven, Rowan's arms wrapped around her from behind. The now-familiar rush of adrenaline hit her along with the heady scent of his spicy cologne. When he leaned in closer to place a kiss on the column of her neck, her body buzzed with desire. Oh, this man; there was something about him that thrilled and excited her. It wasn't just one thing about him, but everything. The way he touched, the way he kissed, the way he fit right into her family. The way they fit together.

"Good morning." She turned in his arms to press a kiss against his lips. "And Merry Christmas."

"Merry Christmas." Then he said words that would have her fall in love with him if she wasn't already. "Do you need some help?"

"Yes, please. I told my sister I'd make them all this wonderful Christmas breakfast just like our family cook used to make."

"You won't have to do it by yourself. That's why you have me."

They worked together, which made it all go so much faster, and before long they had the table set, complete with a big hearty plate of bacon, eggs, potatoes and flapjacks.

"Don't forget this." In the center of the table, Rowan placed the platter of cookies from last night, still wrapped. "Probably shouldn't unwrap these until after the kids are finished eating."

"Sure, but I'm a grown-up." Allison fished under the plastic and grabbed a tea cookie, taking a bite.

"You little sneak." Rowan made as if to grab it from her hand, but she offered him a taste. "Hmm. At least you're generous."

From behind them, someone cleared their throat and when she turned, Billy stood there, one teenage son on either side of him. Rowan made no move to put space between them. Instead, his fingers slid down her arm to hold her hand.

"Merry Christmas," Billy said, and Branson and Nicky did the same.

"Wow, look at this!" Nicky gravitated toward the table.

"Did you cook all this, Aunt Allison?" Branson said.

"Yes, with Rowan's help." She brushed a hint of powdered sugar from the side of his mouth.

"Charlotte will be thrilled," Billy said. "I was just going to bring her up some oatmeal."

"I'm sick of oatmeal!"

Charlotte appeared in the doorway, looking bedraggled and wiped out. There were bags under her poor sister's eyes.

"Babe, I was bringing you breakfast in bed, remember?" Billy draped his arm around her.

"My back hurts and I can't lie down anymore."

"Look at this," Billy said, pointing to the table. "Allison and Rowan went all out. We're having a countrified breakfast."

"Thank you, sissy." Charlotte waddled up to Allison and hugged her then embraced Rowan. "And, Rowan, if I haven't said so before, you're a prince among men."

Jill ran into the kitchen so fast, she partially slid across the floor in her socks. "What did I miss? Are we opening presents yet?"

"First, breakfast!" Allison spread her arms and ushered everyone to the table.

They descended on the food like a pack of wolves, or perhaps more like bears who'd come out of hibernation.

"Stop!" Charlotte said and everyone turned to her. "We have to say the blessing first."

"Right," Billy said, and they all held hands as they gave thanks.

For the next few minutes, conversation was light as everyone seemed too busy chewing. A good sign.

Then Nicky pointed to the cookie tray. "Where did those cookies come from?"

"Your Aunt Allison got them for you," Rowan said with a grin.

Allison sat up straighter, ready for her medal. "Rowan and I went to Aunt Eloise and Uncle Dante's cookie exchange, and this is what we brought home."

"You mean you just show up to this exchange and they *give* you cookies? Why didn't I ever know about this?" Branson said, sneaking his hand under the plastic wrap to take one.

"No, dummy," Jill said. "You have to *bring* cookies, too. That's the exchange part."

"It's official," Charlotte said. "Allison, you win Christmas!"

"Why, thank you." Allison went hand to chest.

"Speech! Speech!" Nicky said.

"Thank you all so very much. I would like to thank the Academy…" Allison said. "Sorry, I have always wanted to say that."

Everyone laughed, but none harder than Rowan.

"It's Christmas Day, so I have one important and possibly life-changing question." Rowan spread his hands to indicate everyone at the table. "You don't have to answer if you're not comfortable, but is *Die Hard* a Christmas movie, yes or no?"

"Totally a Christmas movie," Branson said, and he and Nicky fist-bumped.

"Wait," Allison said. "Is this going to be split down male and female lines?"

"No way," Jill said. "It's totally a Christmas movie. Bruce Willis attends a Christmas party! There's music, and a tree, and presents. I mean, c'mon!"

"And a lot of violence," Charlotte said with a wince.

"Well, in *It's a Wonderful Life*, there's a war!" Nicky said. "You don't get any more violent than that."

"Okay, okay, point taken," Billy said.

Never mind the "war" wasn't showed in the movie, Allison had to agree to a point.

"What side do you fall on in this?" Rowan nudged her.

"Fine!" Allison raised her palms in an "I give up" motion. "It's a Christmas movie."

She received a round of applause.

A few minutes later, the kids announced it was time for presents. Though there'd been a gift name exchange so the kids wouldn't break their banks, Branson had a gift for everyone. Of course, all of it was University of Montana gear.

Rowan immediately put on his U of M silver-and-maroon beanie cap and looked adorable.

Then he opened the present she'd bought him.

"I get it," he said as he held up the gift. "For casino night!"

It was all she could find with special meaning. A set of chips and cards to commemorate his joke about how he'd been managing her apartment while she'd been gone.

"Casino night?" Charlotte asked.

"Private joke," they both said at once.

They had one other private joke: their neighbor, Mrs. Havisham.

Charlotte opened a gift from Billy, a pair of diamond earrings that had to have set him back.

"Oh my God, Billy. I love these!" She kissed her husband sweetly.

Once again, Allison was reminded of how every love story happened in its own time. Charlotte and Billy had been apart for years and, for her part, Allison never dreamed they'd ever be back together again. And yet she could see so clearly how well they belonged together, like they were made for each other.

Jill, who'd appointed herself the dispenser of presents from under the tree, gave Allison a small package. "This one says it's for you."

To Allison.

From Rowan.

She immediately recognized the brightly colored wrapping paper and stickers from Sadie's Holiday House that meant he must have gone back later without her. The box was small, which usually meant jewelry, but she didn't want to get ahead of herself. She already had a beautiful ring from him. Tearing into the wrapping paper, she gently lifted the lid. Inside was a golden locket in the shape of an envelope. The front was engraved with the words *Air Mail.* Taking it out of the box, she held it by the long chain.

She'd asked him to pick up her mail while she was gone. The gift was sentimental, special, and showed her a great deal of thought. Rowan had actually picked out a far more heartfelt gift than she'd managed to do. As she traced each letter, the locket suddenly slid open like an actual envelope to reveal another message inside. This one said *I love you.*

I love you. He'd said it first, with a gift she'd never forget. This present held far more meaning for her than anything he could have given her, including a ring. It was his heart, given open and freely to her, when she'd been keeping hers locked up tight.

She wanted to cry with relief that she hadn't imagined anything. These emotions between them were all as real as she'd hoped.

She stood and walked toward him. "Thank you."

He put his arms around her, tightly, pulling her close. "You're welcome."

The entire Abernathy clan stopped what they were doing to watch. Allison could feel their gazes boring into her. When she hugged Rowan, she looked over her shoulder and caught Charlotte and Billy exchanging confused looks. Were she and Rowan together for real? Or still pretending? No wonder they were confused. Allison wanted to shout to the world that she was in love, and it had all started with a little white lie.

She was about to say those very words when the doorbell rang.

"Who could that be?" Billy said, getting up to answer the door.

"Whoever it is, I'm sorry, but I'm not in the mood for company," Charlotte said, rubbing her back. "I need some more Tylenol."

"I'll get it." Jill ran out of the room.

"Are you feeling okay, Charlotte?" Allison said. "You don't look too well rested."

Her whole demeanor seemed different this morning and now distracted Allison. The pregnancy had been rough on her sister and Allison wasn't sure how she'd make it to her scheduled C-section. She'd tried her best to lighten her sister's load, but maybe everything she'd done hadn't been enough.

Charlotte clapped a hand to her forehead. "Actually, I think I'm going to skip out on the big holiday celebration today at Mom and Dad's."

"No one will blame you. We'll figure something out. I'll stay with you and Billy can take the kids."

"I'll be fine," Charlotte said, pulling up her blanket. "You go and bring me back some of Mom's apple cranberry crunch. And some cranberry walnut cake. Oh, and don't forget the apple cinnamon."

The kids laughed.

"What?" asked Charlotte. "It's the only time of the year Mom actually bakes anything, and her stuff is so good I wish she'd do it more often. I crave it all year!"

"We'll bring you one of each," Branson said.

"We have company." Billy reappeared in the living room carrying a large, wrapped present.

Allison's eyes widened when she saw Perri standing next to Billy, carrying a large gift bag brimming with even more presents.

Allison didn't think it was her imagination when Rowan took a step back from her. The shock of seeing Perri in her sister's home, in this scenario, rendered Allison speechless. Her stomach dropped. She almost felt as if she'd done something wrong and had been caught in the act, when nothing could be further from the truth. Rowan was a single man. At least, according to him.

"Hey, everyone! Hi, Allison." Perri dropped her bag of gifts. "Rowan. Hello."

"What are you *doing* here?" he asked her.

"I called your mother to wish her a Merry Christmas and she told me you were visiting Allison and her family in Montana. I couldn't stay away." Perri turned to Allison's family, most of whom were giving her curious gazes. "Please excuse me for intruding. But Christmas is a time of reconciliation, don't you think? It makes you realize who and what you love. Perspective. I know I sure needed some."

Yes, she usually did. And it was just as Allison suspected. Perri was going to try to slide back into Rowan's life as if a breakup had never happened.

Jill walked into the room with the bottle of Tylenol. "Hello. Who are you?"

"I'm Perri. Rowan's girlfriend." She smiled, bright as the evening star.

Allison noticed Billy cringe and Charlotte cover her face in obvious sympathy.

"*Ex*-girlfriend," Rowan said a moment too late for Allison.

"Oh, we just had a little fight." Perri waved her hands dismissively. "We do that a lot but then we can never stay away from each other for long."

Allison's heart jerked and spasmed with anticipated pain. This was her worst fear come to life. Perri had officially changed her mind, wanted Rowan back, and was already here to claim him. On Christmas Day of all things. Worse, how was Rowan supposed to let her down gently? Assuming he *wanted* to, that was. She didn't have any doubts the feelings he'd expressed for Allison recently were real, but this was a living, breathing reminder of his past. Of home. Seattle, where they'd be going back after this brief interlude. He saw before him his past and his possible future.

They might both be Perri.

Maybe they, and all this, had simply been a wonderful little dream.

"Um, Perri," Rowan said, "we were just celebrating Christmas with the Abernathy family."

"Yes, and I do apologize, but I brought gifts for everyone."

The kids' faces brightened, as if they needed any more presents after their haul.

"And I got a room for us at the Heights Hotel because I know it must be cramped here with all of you!" Perri said this as if she were doing them all a great big favor.

"That's kind, but…well…let's go outside and talk for a minute." Rowan led her, hand on the small of her back, toward the front door. "Folks, I'll be right back."

The door shut and the quiet seemed suddenly deafening. All eyes were on Allison, waiting for her to…do what? Fall apart? Cry? Throw herself at Rowan and beg him not to go back to his ex?

"Somebody *say* something." Allison flopped back on the couch.

"I don't think this is my size," Jill said, holding up a sweater.

"You can return it," Charlotte said. "Allison, what's going on? I thought you and Rowan—"

"I don't want to talk about it."

"Don't worry, Aunt Allison," Branson said. "A lot of guys don't go for women like her. They prefer a good personality."

Oh joy.

Billy gave his son the parental stare-down and poor Branson wilted under it.

"I think you're beautiful," Jill said softly. "And smart, which is more important anyway."

Allison appreciated Jill now more than ever.

"You are beautiful in *every* way," Charlotte said. "And if Rowan can't see it, that's *his* problem."

"You guys… I mean, he's just *talking* to her," Nicky said. "Geez."

But the "talking" became louder as they were right outside the front door on the porch.

"Are you *cheating* on me? With *Allison*?" Perri could be heard saying.

"I thought that was his ex," said Branson.

"It is," Allison said. "I guess she's having a difficult time letting go."

Outside, Rowan and Perri moved farther away from the door and couldn't be heard any longer.

Thank you, God.

"Let's talk about something else, okay?" Charlotte said. "Like how huge I am. And how tired of being pregnant I am."

"But we talk about that every day." Billy smirked.

"Did you decide on a name yet?" Jill said.

"No," Charlotte and Billy said at once.

"But there are lots of heavy contenders," Billy said. "I think we've narrowed down the list. Especially on a boy's name. Eric."

The kids started shouting out more names, for a boy and a girl, some of them ridiculous, and it was almost enough to take her attention away from what was obviously happening outside.

Finally, after several minutes, Rowan walked inside. Alone.

He grabbed his coat. "Allison, can I talk to you for a minute?"

Feeling a ball of needles settling in her throat, Allison led him into the kitchen. The same kitchen where they'd bonded over baking cookies. The place where they'd first kissed. The place where this morning he'd wrapped his arms around her like he would never let her go. They'd been so domestic. Comfortable. Like a real couple.

She almost didn't want to hear what he had to say next. He was going to shatter this little bubble of hers with a few words.

"First, I had no idea she was coming here," he whispered.

"I figured." She lowered her head, not wanting to meet his gaze and see the regret in them.

He would no doubt hate the idea of hurting her, but Allison should have known better than to get in the middle of this on-again, off-again dance. It was her own damn fault for taking a risk. Her damn fault for not keeping what was pretend right where it should be.

And above all else, her own fault for letting her heart get involved.

"It was incredibly rude of her to just barge in like this and I apologize on her behalf. Sometimes, she…well, her insecurities cause her to make rash decisions."

And there it was. It sounded as though he were defending her.

"I understand."

"I'm going to have to talk to her. I think I should take her back to the hotel."

"Oh."

Back to the hotel. That didn't sound like a good idea to Allison. It didn't sound like a good idea at all.

"She says she wants us to get *married*. The breakup made her realize that I'm her end game."

For a moment, Allison was speechless. This moment was turning into her worst nightmare. Previously her worst thought was that when she'd return to Seattle she'd find Perri had moved in with him. Now she wanted to *marry* Rowan?

"Allison?" Rowan said. "Did you *hear* me?"

"I heard you. She wants to marry you. That's…well, I gotta say, that's pretty shocking." Allison stood back, trying not to touch him.

It seemed particularly dangerous to touch him now. If she reached for him, she might take him by the shoulders and shake him, remind him that not long ago they had tentative plans to be together.

Remind him that just a few minutes ago he'd given her a locket with the words "I love you" on it!

"Tell me about it. I don't know who or what gave her the idea. She said she's frustrated that I never asked her to marry me even after two years of dating. She hoped it would be this year and when I didn't show any indication I was shopping for rings, she gave up."

"And now that she thinks you've moved on, she can't stand it."

"I swear that I didn't encourage her in any way."

She tipped her chin. "Not in a way you were aware of anyway."

"What's that supposed to mean?"

Unless Perri was unhinged, maybe Rowan had inadvertently said something to encourage her. Or maybe, just by being a good guy again, he was sending her mixed signals. Either way, Allison didn't want to be a part of this.

"It means I don't see how she got to the point of believing she could just show up here and you'd take her back. There's a reason. You've somehow…allowed this."

"No way. I'm not allowing it."

"Maybe you should."

The words were bitter, and she didn't mean them for a second. It was as if her brain was making decisions without her.

Constructing a barricade around her heart.

Rowan blinked. "What? *Why?*"

"I think deep down this is what you want. How will you know you can move on otherwise?"

"Allison, is that what *you* really want?" Rowan shook his head, scowling.

"Well, I don't think she should stay here. It's my sister's house, and—"

"That's…not what I meant."

She didn't know what he wanted from her. If she had

a temper tantrum like a child, insisting he call Perri an Uber instead of driving her himself, she'd be childish. She'd sound unreasonable. Insisting she go with them would be awkward and smack of jealousy, doubt and insecurity. But the truth was she didn't *want* him to take Perri back to the hotel. Allison could see how Perri would manipulate the situation further once she was alone with Rowan.

And because Allison was in love with him, everything had changed. All her old insecurities had come home to roost.

She couldn't tell him she loved him...not now. He had a choice to make. If he was truly done with his ex, this was the moment of truth.

"I... I don't know what you want me to say. If you want to take her back to the hotel to talk, I guess I understand. You have a lot to discuss."

"Not that much. She's *not* going to interfere with everything we have planned for today."

This was kind of him, as he understood they'd be going to her family's holiday party and he should be in attendance. It was an important appearance in their charade.

"Okay. You take her back to the hotel and explain everything. Tell her we were just having fun. You were trying to help me out with my controlling parents. I'm sure she'll understand."

"Is that what you want me to say?"

No! I want you to say, "Goodbye, Perri. I've fallen deeply in love with Allison and we're going to be together from now on. I'm never going to marry you. I didn't mean to hurt you."

She couldn't say the words out loud. She couldn't beg. Taylor women didn't beg.

Allison crossed her arms over her heart. "I think you

should do what you want to do. What you feel is right to deescalate the situation."

"Right." Rowan sighed and dragged a hand through his hair. "Well, I'm going to the family party with you. I won't let you down."

"Okay."

She waited a beat to see if he'd hug her or kiss her good-bye. It felt like a wall stood between them now when just hours ago they'd been all over each other. But when he didn't make a move, she didn't either.

He turned and walked out of the kitchen.

Allison wasn't certain she should hope or even expect him to come back.

And she wasn't sure she wanted him to either.

Chapter Eighteen

Rowan couldn't believe this.

First, Perri's timing.

Second, her proposal! *Seriously?*

Third, Allison.

Allison.

His heart had crashed and burned when she suggested he do whatever he wanted to do, as if it didn't matter to her one way or another.

He'd whisked Perri away from the Abernathy house as fast as he could. Rowan hadn't even looked at Billy and Charlotte. What must they think of him? They probably thought he was playing two women against each other, and one of them was their sister. He'd be lucky if they allowed him back in the house. Both Billy and Charlotte were protective of Allison and he didn't blame them. He also felt protective over her, and the look of confusion and hurt on her face had killed him.

But he was hurt, too. Hurt and disappointed. He'd given Allison plenty of opportunities to tell him she loved him. She hadn't taken a single one. The gift he'd given her *said* he loved her. He couldn't have been clearer. But she obviously still had doubts. At this point, he didn't know if they were about Perri anymore.

Maybe the person she really doubted was him.

One of the things he loved and admired most about Allison was her sense of security in herself. She understood who she was and wouldn't try to be anyone else or play games. When she'd sent him away, it was tough to believe insecurity had anything to do with it. And then he remembered the old relationships she'd told him about. How just as she was ready to let her guard down, she learned a boyfriend had lost patience and moved on to find someone with less defenses. He had to find a way to prove to her that would never be him. He'd have all the patience in the world for her to get to where he was with her.

At least he had one thing going for him. The gift. She'd seen it. It wasn't just a simple necklace. It had a message. There could be no doubt as to his feelings. He told himself this would all blow over when he got back to the Abernathy ranch.

Snow was still falling as he drove Perri to town in the truck he'd borrowed from Billy. He didn't even dart a look over at Perri when he said, "We need to talk."

"Look, I'm sorry I ruined their Christmas, but now we can take the entire afternoon to discuss our future." She turned a bit to face him. "Please, please, *please* give me another chance. I know I blew it. But everyone deserves a second chance."

"And you've had plenty of second chances. Look, I don't want to get married."

Not to Perri. No matter how hard he'd tried to talk himself into the idea, he'd known for a while they had issues that would never be overcome. They wanted different things. He had no idea how they'd stayed together so long. The shocking truth that hit him now was that he hadn't thought he deserved any better. He'd been so wrong.

"You won't even think about it?" From the sound of her voice, Perri was beyond frustrated and halfway to angry. "How is that fair to me? At least consider it! Are you telling me I wasted two years of my life with you?"

"I'm sorry, but I don't love you. It's over, Perri. We went over this. We're not even together anymore. That was your decision."

"I wasn't serious about that, and I regret it. You know me. I get frustrated by your lack of commitment. We're both not getting any younger, you know, and I thought at thirty-six you'd be ready to settle down. It's confusing. You send me mixed messages. I thought I'd have a ring by now. We've been dating two years. Two *years*!"

"I wonder if we put all of our breakups together if we'd even average an entire year."

She dismissed his comment. "You're exaggerating."

"I'm not. Either way, it doesn't matter. We're done. This isn't going to work, no matter what we do, because we're not right for each other. I don't think we ever were."

"I think we *are* right for each other!" she rebuked. Then her tone softened. "Maybe we should try premarital counseling."

Rowan could just see that. The counselor would laugh them out of the office.

He should have been better prepared for this. Allison had warned him, and he hadn't listened. He hadn't believed Perri could be this desperate to hang on to him. At the very least, he'd thought she'd wait until he'd returned home to try to get him back. It was his fault, he realized, for being far too nice. He saw in Perri a desperate kind of insecurity he recognized from his own past. But it wasn't his job to heal her. He would have to let go of his need to help people, including people who didn't want to be helped.

He drew a deep breath then said, "I've made up my mind and I'm moving on. I'm sorry."

"So, how long have you been attracted to Allison? Why didn't you tell me?" Perri swung right into bitterness and jealousy.

He could tell her the truth, but it was also none of her business. This was the time to establish boundaries. His love life, what might be left of it after this, was not Perri's concern. She couldn't understand if he told her that, for the first time in his life, he understood what it was like to be in love. He now had firsthand experience with the inability to stop thinking about someone, day or night. He now understood what it was like to wake up with someone on your mind, and to fall asleep with them still there, too. It was true what people said: falling in love was basically like being a sixteen-year-old again.

These were all things he'd never once experienced with Perri, not even in those early days of romance.

His feelings toward Allison were best kept to himself. So, he simply said, "We're not talking about her."

"Oh, so that's how it is!" Perri crossed her arms and turned away from him. "I can't believe you!"

They didn't speak the rest of the way.

Ever the gentleman, when they reached Heights Hotel, Rowan carried Perri's suitcase inside the lobby of the hotel. The brightly decorated lobby didn't look cheerful through his eyes. The mood for him now was heavily *The Nightmare Before Christmas.*

He walked her to the elevator and waited for the doors to open. He wheeled her suitcase in and she stepped inside. As the doors began to slide closed, Perri stuck her arm between them.

"Aren't you coming up?" Her eyes were shimmering, her lower lip quivering.

"No. I'm not. I think you'll be fine from here."

"Rowan, the truth is I was only insecure because of the way you always talked about Allison. She seemed to be on your mind, and it seemed sometimes that you valued her opinions more than mine. Even though I know you loved me, and you were with me, it didn't feel that way. Just think of how that made me feel."

"I did love you, and I really tried." He lowered his head then gave her one last look filled with regret. "I'm sorry, Perri. I hope we can be friends because I care about you."

She let the elevator doors close without saying another word.

He turned and walked back outside into the heavily falling snow.

There was still a way to salvage this day. Glancing at his phone, he calculated that he'd been gone well over thirty minutes, a result of his driving while distracted by his encounter with Perri. With this snowfall, it would take him even longer to get back. But he'd get back, talk to Allison, and get ready for the Taylor party tonight. It all seemed within reach. He'd actually tell Allison he loved her instead of letting a necklace pendant do it for him. After all, what if she hadn't slid the locket open to see the inscription inside? She might have thought he'd simply given her an envelope locket. Well, either way, he'd tell her tonight that he couldn't live without her.

Rowan didn't know if he'd been driving two minutes or two hours because, in this snowfall, he'd begun to lose perspective. But somewhere around mile marker five, the truck slid off the road.

He cursed a blue streak. Unbelievable. He was having a run of bad luck after an incredible one of good fortune. So, by his calculations, he was now midway between the Heights Hotel and the Abernathy ranch.

He pulled out his phone and texted Allison.

On my way back and will explain all when I get there. I had a little mishap. Truck slid off the road.

He waited a few seconds for her reply, either via words or exclamation emojis. She'd have someone on the way to get him immediately, he was certain. Either that, or he was going to have to walk to the ranch.

He sent another text.

I'm going to push the truck out of this ditch. Should work. Right? What could go wrong?

A full five minutes later, Allison still had not responded. There were not even the bubbles indicating she was composing a reply. But she was probably too angry and disappointed with him to find words. It wasn't his fault Perri had showed up, but Allison had been right all along. Perri still wanted him. But, after today, he had a feeling she'd finally received the message. Now, he'd seen what a healthy relationship looked like, and a future with Allison was what he craved. What he wanted more than anything.

If he had still loved Perri, he would not have let this attraction to Allison grow the way it had. More to the point, it shouldn't have had a chance to even take a foothold.

Now, if only he could know for certain that Allison felt the same way about him.

He sent one last text.

Don't give up on me. I'll be there to take you to the party or die trying.

Chapter Nineteen

So, Rowan had left with Perri. Oh sure, he'd said it was to take her to the hotel, but Perri wanted to get *married*. Married! Allison didn't have any doubts that she'd do her best to get Rowan back. If Rowan's mind could be swayed that easily, then she didn't want him.

Unfortunately, this wasn't the truth. She very much wanted him. Forever.

And the idea petrified her.

This wouldn't end well. She felt it in the marrow of her bones.

Allison ran up the steps to her bedroom where she could cry in private. She was terribly embarrassed by all of this. The kids had heard Perri claim to be Rowan's girlfriend. He'd corrected her, sure, but somewhat half-heartedly, in Allison's opinion. Seeing Perri again might have been the only thing he'd needed to realize he still had feelings for her. He should, and probably would, let Allison down easily, once he returned to the house.

If he returned.

Allison couldn't fault him for doing the right thing and taking Perri to the hotel. It was classic Rowan. A good guy. He was still doing his best to help Allison, too, and they had the Taylor party tonight. He would not let her down. She had to remember that.

Wiping away her tears, she sat on the bed and fingered the locket again. Was it possible he hadn't even realized the message was inside the locket? Maybe he'd been in such a hurry that he'd bought and paid for it without realizing he'd accidentally told her he loved her? The point being, he hadn't said the words out loud. Neither had she, for that matter, though she'd been about to. And she would be forever grateful for the timing of that doorbell saving her from further humiliation.

She'd been alone in her room all of ten minutes when there was a knock on her door.

Charlotte entered the room, her face puffy and pink with exertion.

"What are you doing?" Allison said. "Why did you come up here? I could have come downstairs. Can I get you something?"

"I need the exercise. Believe it or not, I suddenly have all this energy. Sure, I'm carrying a lot more weight around than normal, but I'm tired of sitting on my behind all day." Either way, she waddled right to the twin bed and sat down with a little gasp. "My back is the problem now, not my energy level. So...what's going on with you? It's not like you to hide away like this."

"I'm feeling sorry for myself when I have no business doing that. I had a bad sense this was coming." Allison sniffed and wiped away a tear. "I should have been prepared."

"You knew his ex would show up uninvited to someone's private family celebration?" Charlotte spoke through a tight jaw and gritted teeth.

She was clearly very angry on Allison's behalf.

"I *told* you she wasn't going to let him go."

"Yes, you did. But he has something to do with all this. What makes you think *he's* going to give her another chance?"

"History?"

"Yes, but he's never been with you before. That has given him new perspective."

It sounded very optimistic, and exactly the encouraging words Allison would expect from her big sister.

"I'd like to think so, but who knows?"

"You'll find out when he comes back in a few minutes and explains everything. He really cares about you, and I can see you've developed some real feelings for him."

"I fell in love with him." Allison choked back a sob. "I never thought it could be like this, not this overwhelming feeling that suddenly I can't live without him. It's scary."

"Oh, I remember. Terrifying. When you can't live without someone, you have to wonder what happens if they have no trouble living without *you*."

"Exactly."

"It happened fast for you two, but that's how it is sometimes. I still remember the first time I laid eyes on Billy. Though I didn't even know what to call it at the time because I was so young, now I think it was definitely love. That hot, kablammy, fireworks feeling that your life has changed forever because of one person."

"I've always wanted what you and Billy have."

"And you will have it, Allison." Charlotte patted her sister's leg.

"Probably not with Rowan."

"Don't be so sure." Charlotte bent over. "Oh, my back. I've never had back *pain* like this. I… I think…oh, God. No."

"Charlotte? What is it? Talk to me!"

"It...can't be." Her face was frozen, her eyes bulging, her forehead breaking out in a sweat. "But I think my water just broke."

Everything happened fast after that.

Allison frantically called for Billy, who came running upstairs as if the house were on fire. "Charlotte!"

"I'm sorry. I feel so dumb. I was probably in labor this whole time, but it was pain wrapping around my back, not cramps, like I expected. I didn't even recognize I'm in labor. I don't want to have a baby on Christmas Day! Think of the pressure on the poor kid."

"It's a great day to be born. Hey, look at it this way. Everyone is already celebrating," Allison said, emphasizing the positive as her sister had just done for her.

Charlotte half moaned, half groaned.

Billy raked his fingers through his hair. "I should have called the doctor. I've been worried about you for days." He leaned out the door and yelled, "Branson! Go fire up Charlotte's truck. Hurry up! We're going to the hospital. Now!"

Jill squealed and came running upstairs. "Oh my gawd! It's *happening*? Hang on, I need my phone."

"No phone!" Billy and Charlotte said at once.

"What's happening?" Nicky said from behind Jill.

"She's having the baby!" Jill threw her hands up.

"Like, *now*?" Nicky said. "On *Christmas*?"

Billy managed to carry Charlotte down the steps in his arms. She was still in her pajamas and robe, so Allison grabbed her coat and boots. The kids quickly dressed in winter gear because the snow was now coming down harder. It would take longer to get to the hospital.

But they had to get there, and soon.

Allison and Billy sat in the middle row seat of the SUV, one on either side of Charlotte.

"Drive carefully, Branson," Billy barked. "We don't want to slide off the road."

"Why did you say that? I'm already nervous," Branson said.

"You're not going to slide off," Allison said, trying to give their driver some comfort. "Don't worry."

"You better not. I don't want to get out in this snow and dig," Nicky said from the back.

As if this was their biggest problem. Digging. Allison could hear the sounds of his video game. Oh to be so unconcerned and blasé about a woman in labor! He must not have heard the news of babies sometimes being delivered in cars en route to the hospital. At the moment, Allison was trying to vanquish each of those stories from her mind by shutting her eyes tightly.

"You're not going to have the baby in the car, are you?" Jill turned from the passenger front seat with a look of sheer terror on her face. "I don't want my baby sister born in a car on the side of the road!"

"Jilly Bean, I am equally invested in that scenario. Believe me," Charlotte huffed.

"Wait," Billy said softly. "We're having a *girl*?"

"Oops!" Jill laughed. "I'm sorry, Dad."

"Look at this way. You were going to find out in a few hours anyway," Branson said. "And there's a fifty-fifty chance it's either one. I don't see what the big deal is."

"I've known the whole time and kept it quiet," Jill said. "Charlotte only told *me* since Dad wanted to be surprised and she knows I can keep a secret."

Charlotte groaned. "Please get me to the hospital."

"Everyone shut up back there! I'm trying to concentrate!" Branson yelled.

Quiet ensued, punctuated only by Charlotte's groans and Billy's soft whispers of encouragement.

A few minutes later, Allison sat in the Labor and Delivery waiting room with the kids.

She was going to text Rowan that the party was off tonight, which would suddenly release him from at least that obligation. But she realized in all the chaos that she'd forgotten her phone at the house. It could wait, she told herself. He'd go back to the house, which in their haste they'd left unlocked, and make himself at home.

"Allison!" Her mother rushed over to them. "We ran right over when Billy phoned."

Both Imogen and her father were still decked out in the formal wear they'd donned for the party before the baby news.

"What timing." Thaddeus shook his head. "Now our party is ruined."

"Thad! The most important thing is Charlotte," Imogen chastised him. "She's early and I just hope the baby is okay."

"I'm sure she and the baby will both be fine," Allison said, though she wasn't sure of any such thing.

They'd called the doctor, who'd said he might now have to deliver naturally. And that would be difficult, considering the baby had been in a breach position at Charlotte's last couple of appointments. Allison wasn't sure how all this worked, and she didn't want to ask to borrow a phone and do an online search to get a fast medical degree. Sometimes ignorance was bliss.

"I don't have any information for you," Allison told her parents. "She and Billy are back there. That's all I know."

"Have a seat, Thad." Her mother pointed to an empty seat near Branson. "We might be here for a while."

"Where's that fiancé of yours, Allison?" her father said, taking a seat and straightening his jacket. "I don't see him around. Did he already take off on you?"

The words were like a poison-tipped arrow, since she worried her father might be right this time. But, as God was her witness, she would not admit defeat in front of her father!

"Absolutely not! He—"

"He had to go take his girlfriend to her hotel," Nicky said with the emotional intelligence of a six-year-old.

Branson elbowed him hard in the gut.

"What?" Nicky said as if waking up from a dream.

"*Ex*-girlfriend!" Jill said.

"Allison sure can pick 'em." Thaddeus snorted and shook his head.

"I'm right here, Dad!" Allison held her arms open.

"Maybe now you'll give a good man another chance. Frederick is still available and has plenty of his own money. You don't seem to realize that some of these men you pick might just want you for your money."

"Why? Because I have nothing *else* to offer?"

"No, no, of course you have so much to offer the right man," her mother said. "Thad. Shut. Up."

"I'm only trying to help. She only comes home once a year and this is my chance to straighten her out," her father said.

"Don't you mean marry me off to one of your friends?"

"He's a fine man," Thaddeus said.

Allison didn't know how much more of her father she could take. "Maybe it's best if I don't come home again next year. Would that be better?"

"No, of course not!" Her mother stepped between them and shot her father a glare. "We always want you home."

Thankfully, Billy's parents, Bonnie and Asa, showed up then and put an end to the Taylor argument.

"How's the baby?" Bonnie Abernathy wanted to know.

"We're waiting to hear," Allison's mother explained.

"What a terrible night to have to rush to the hospital." Bonnie wrung her hands together.

Before much longer, they were fielding calls from the rest of the Taylor and Abernathy clans who wanted to brave the snow and come to support Charlotte and Billy and see the baby when it was born. They now had a full house, both the Taylors and the Abernathys taking over the entire waiting room.

"We could be here for a while, you know," Bonnie said. "I'd say the kids should go back home but the snow is awfully bad out there. Best to stay off the road."

This was true, and Allison wondered whether the snow would force Rowan to stick it out at the Heights Hotel with Perri. Snowbound together. How romantic. The idea sickened her.

But if he'd truly dropped Perri off, he should have been on his way back at least an hour ago. However, if he'd engaged in even a little bit of conversation with Perri, he might have been caught in the storm. Allison had to put an end to these thoughts. There was no point in turning this over and over in her mind, but as she paced the floor, she couldn't stop. She wandered the hospital, going to the closed gift shop and doing a little window-shopping. Finding the coffee machine, she brought coffees to everyone, and hot chocolate for the kids.

Outside, the grounds had been transformed into a blanket of white. Car hoods were covered with a thick layer of snow. It was truly a white Christmas, just not the way they'd all pictured it. She'd pictured being cozy inside by the fireplace, roasting marshmallows, not walking the halls of a badly lit hospital corridor.

Finally, Billy appeared in the waiting room, grinning from ear to ear.

"It's a girl," he announced. "And she's healthy. Small, about six pounds, but healthy, the doctor says."

"And Charlotte?" Imogen said.

"She's great. A real champ. She didn't think she'd have a chance to deliver naturally, but apparently the baby turned sometime during the night."

"Wonderful!" Bonnie said. "It will be a faster recovery for Charlotte."

Just like that, Allison's thoughts were back to Rowan and how he'd screwed up with his lack of knowledge on C-sections. She couldn't blame him. Now, she could laugh, remembering Rowan's earnest but slightly confused expression. And then, more importantly, the way he'd claimed her. Or so it had seemed to her at the time. But maybe it had been less of a romantic claiming than a way to salvage his own bruised ego. Funny how she was seeing everything in a different light now. What she wanted versus what was *real*. They were often not one and the same. At least, not for her.

"When can we see her?" Imogen asked.

"What's her name?" Jill demanded. "Do you have one? You never told us what you decided! Beyoncé is still a great name."

"You'll name my grandchild after a celebrity over my dead body," Thaddeus said.

"That could be arranged," Jill said softly where possibly only Allison could hear.

It made her smile and want to kiss Jill. Thankfully, Billy

was her father, but *this* girl was never going to let any man tell her what to do.

Branson chuckled. "Or what about Taylor? Her name could be *Taylor* Abernathy."

"Now you're talking!" Thaddeus pointed, not realizing the boy wanted to name her after the beautiful singer and not the family's name.

"Oh, what a perfect marriage of both family names," Bonnie said.

"Nah. It should be a Christmas kind of name," Asa Abernathy said. "Like Eve. Or Holly."

"Well, it's just like you to want to leave my name out. But we already have a Christmastime grandchild and Merry is taken," Thaddeus grumbled.

"Charlotte and I still haven't decided." Billy held up his palms.

"Oh my gawd, what are you waiting for? For her to start *kindergarten*?" Jill scowled and crossed her arms.

Billy rolled his eyes. "Okay, well, who would like to go back and see them? They're in a private room. Only one at a time."

What ensued was similar to the mad old days of the after–Thanksgiving Day sales that had resulted in injury and mayhem. Everyone rushed Billy, but Allison literally elbowed her way to the front.

"I think we can all agree I should be first."

"But what about me?" Her mother went hand to chest. "I'm the *grandmother*."

"And so am *I*," Bonnie said.

Allison held her ground, ready to prevent the Battle of the Grandmas. "Too bad, only one at a time, and I'd hate for Billy to have to decide between you. I'm the *auntie* and at the moment there's only one here, so I win."

Fortunately, Eloise, or Billy's sister, Robin, hadn't yet arrived so that made Allison the reigning Aunt. Allison squared her shoulders and followed a smirking Billy toward Charlotte's room.

Billy held out his arm at the doorway for Allison to go through first.

Then he announced, "Here's the winner."

Allison took one step inside the room, and everything else stilled. This place felt holy on Christmas night. A streetlight from the parking lot below shone through the window, giving an almost ethereal glow, the snow gently falling outside.

Charlotte wore the smile of the Madonna, holding a tightly wrapped bundle in her arms. She didn't speak. She didn't have to because two sisters could communicate without words.

Charlotte silently revealed to Allison that she was finally holding the baby she'd dreamed about for years. In her eyes, Allison felt the gaze of a woman who now knew that a great loss could later result in a special kind of joy.

From her position, Allison could only see the top of the baby's head, so she stepped closer to her sister's side. A little dark curl of hair softened the baby's pink face. Her eyes were shut tightly, her mouth pursed as if she wasn't ready for all this commotion.

"Welcome to the world, little one." Allison reached to briefly touch the blanket.

"We don't have a name yet, but I'm leaning toward something appropriate," Charlotte said.

"Something sweet, like Eve?"

"Maybe," Charlotte said. "I'm too happy right now to worry about a name. All I know is she's mine. Do you want to hold her?"

Billy came around to help gently move his baby from Charlotte's arms to Allison's.

"She's absolutely gorgeous," Allison said, her voice thick with emotion. "I can't believe only a few hours ago she was safely inside your womb."

The baby girl was wrapped burrito-style, her little arms pinned to her sides, and she continued to sleep as if she meant serious business.

Allison turned to see both parents were watching their baby with adoration in their eyes. Billy had his arm around Charlotte, and she leaned into him. But she didn't look exhausted anymore.

Billy, on the other hand, looked like he'd been dragged through the mud.

"This was a long time coming," Billy said with a sigh.

It was a gentle reminder that even when things didn't work out the first time, that didn't mean they wouldn't eventually. Allison had to remember that.

When she walked back to the waiting room, a line had formed. Somehow, the two grandmothers had come to an agreement because Charlotte's mother was at the head of it, Bonnie behind her.

"You know what? I'm going back to the house now that I know Charlotte and the baby are okay," Allison said.

"In this snow?" Thaddeus challenged. "Eloise and Dante aren't coming because of the snow. That's smart. You're not a good driver. Sit tight and wait."

But she didn't want to sit. Also, she drove fabulously in the snow, thank you very much. Not that her father would ever admit it. She'd done everything she could for her sister, and Charlotte now couldn't be in a safer place. Everything would be all right. She'd been gone for hours and, in the meantime, Rowan was God knew where. Maybe she was a glutton for punishment, but she wanted to know whether or not he'd made his way back to the ranch. If so, he'd be wondering where they'd all gone.

He'd have questions and, after everything he'd done, and how he'd hung in there with her family, she owed him answers.

Chapter Twenty

When after two hours, he still couldn't get any wheel traction to get the truck out of the ditch, Rowan decided to walk. In the snow. It took two minutes before he realized how dangerous this could be, and he went back to the truck. He sat there in the warmth for the next hour, trying to get a cell signal. Then salvation in the form of a truck rolled up next to him.

The driver rolled down his window. "You look like you could use some help, partner."

"I couldn't get traction to get out of the ditch."

"Good on you to wait it out for help. It's too dangerous out there right now. I'd help you pull the truck out, but we don't have the right equipment with us." The back passenger door slid open. "Hop in. Where you headed?"

"The Bonnie B Ranch." Once inside, the welcome heat began to thaw his poor raw hands. The gloves were going in the fire. They were useless.

"I'm Jesse Bandman," the driver said. "These are my brothers, Sam and Harrison."

"Rowan Scott. What brings you guys out in this weather? Heading to a party?"

"You could say that. We're driving to Star, Idaho, for our family's Hanukah celebration."

"I told you we should have left yesterday," the one named Sam grumbled.

"Aw, those forecasters are never right," Jesse said.

"They were this time," the brother named Harrison said.

Jesse shrugged it off. "So what, we'll be driving in the snow part of the way. It's an adventure!"

Thirty minutes later, Rowan had learned all about the brothers and their family. They happened to know both the Abernathys and the Taylors, too. When they pulled up to the Bonnie B, Rowan was so grateful, he wanted to give them some gas money for their troubles. But Jesse and his brothers refused, telling him it had been done clearly out of the goodness of their hearts.

"Thanks, guys," Rowan said. "You probably saved my life."

"You're welcome. The next chance you get, just pass on the good deed. That's all I ask," Jesse said.

"You got it."

"Have a Merry Christmas," the brothers chorused as he exited the vehicle.

"Happy Hanukah!" Rowan waved and watched the truck drive off, the red taillights winking once.

He turned to the house, noticing one of the trucks gone. Hopefully, Allison hadn't gone to the Taylor party without him. Either way, he needed a shower and a chance to freshen up to be presentable enough for a gathering.

The door was unlocked, and the lights were on inside, but the fire was dying out.

First thing, he removed his useless jacket, gloves, and his sad, defeated boots.

"Allison?" Rowan called out. "Hello? Charlotte? Billy?"

Rowan wandered through the house. Everyone seemed to be gone, which meant they'd all gone to the party without him. As for Charlotte and Billy, maybe they were taking a nap in the bedroom. He certainly wasn't going to knock on *their* door. Surely, one of them would have come out when he'd called to let him know where everyone had gone.

He knocked once on the nursery room door where Allison was staying and let himself inside. There, he found the reason she hadn't responded to any of his text messages. Her phone sat on the twin bed where she'd left it, all of his messages unread.

Fine, he'd catch up with them at the Taylor party.

He hopped in the shower and let the hot water run over him, washing away the chill. His hands and feet went from white to pink as the blood began to flow again. After he thawed, he dressed. It was warm and toasty in the house and he wandered downstairs and restarted the fire. Charlotte and Billy would probably appreciate it once they finished their nap.

The phone rang and Rowan hesitated to answer it, but went ahead when no one in the upstairs bedroom picked up after three rings.

"Abernathy residence, Rowan Scott speaking."

"Hello. It's Eloise. I was wondering if you'd heard anything. No one is answering their phone now. I think possibly the storm is affecting some cell reception."

"Heard anything about what? I just got back from an errand, and no one is here."

Eloise laughed. "Oh, you poor thing. At last, someone who knows even less than I do. It's snowing so badly, we decided not to attempt the drive to the hospital. But apparently Charlotte went into labor earlier."

Words failed him. "She...went into *labor*? When?"

It had to have been soon after he'd left.

"I'm not sure. My mother called and said they were canceling the party and driving to the hospital. I just wondered if the baby has been born yet and thought someone at the house might know."

"Allison forgot her phone at the house. They must have had to leave quickly. I'll have someone call you as soon as I hear anything. Right now, I'm the only one here, but thanks for telling me the party is canceled. I was going to head over there."

"Don't. At least you're both spared the Taylor party."

Good thing because he and Allison had to talk. The way she'd let him go tonight with Perri, encouraging him to work things out with her, made him wonder if she'd changed her mind about them. It confused him, because he hadn't seen that kind of change of heart coming—not from her. He'd need to have a talk with her tonight when she got home from the hospital. Surely she'd opened the locket to see the message inside.

He loved her and now he'd prove it to her if she'd only let him.

Rowan hung up with Eloise and straightened the living room of all the detritus of wrapping paper and boxes, throwing some into the fireplace. He made himself useful, and stacked presents on one end of the couch. He rinsed dishes and loaded the dishwasher.

An hour later, the front door opened.

Allison.

She stopped short when she saw him. "You're back. I didn't think… I wasn't sure…"

"Of course I'm here. Where did you think I'd be?"

"With Perri. You left with her." Her chin trembled.

He heard the hurt and pain in her tone and winced.

"Do you *want* me here, Allison? I need to know. Because I sent Perri back home to Seattle. I could go back, too, and maybe I should."

She flinched. "Do you want to go back with her?"

"No. I'll go home, if that's what you want. But it wouldn't be to be with her. I'd have to start trying to get over you somehow." He took a step toward her. "If you want me to go, just say the word. I will. I don't want to overstay my welcome."

"No, I… I don't want you to go." Her voice shook.

"Okay." He needed more than that, but he would take it slow. "How's Charlotte? Is she okay?"

"Yes. She had a baby girl. Name to be determined."

"Congratulations. That's amazing. Eloise called, but I didn't know what to tell her. She's the one who told me you'd all left for the hospital."

"Almost right after you left with Perri, in fact. It was very sudden. Charlotte's water broke and we were all in a panic. That's when the snow started coming down heavy."

"I'm sorry, honey. That must have been so scary for you." His hands slid up and down her arms. "I've been waiting here by myself for a while."

"You have? For how long?"

So, yeah, he'd been gone for hours, but that was because he'd driven off the road, tried to get out of a ditch, and had to walk part of the way back. He could see what it might look like to Allison. As if maybe he'd spent the afternoon in a hotel room with Perri instead of nearly becoming Frosty the Snowman.

"Actually I've been gone for hours."

"I see." She took off her jacket and hung it on the rack nearby.

"No, you don't see." He strode up to her, planting himself in front of Allison. "I left with Perri, but I was waiting for some kind of signal from you. I expected you to tell me that you didn't want me to go. But you didn't. You actually *encouraged* me to leave."

He tensed, his pulse kicking up a notch or two. If she wanted him to go, he'd have to listen. But first she'd need to say those words to his face.

"I'm sorry, but I didn't want to pressure you any more than I already have. I didn't want to ask for anything more. From the beginning, you've been doing everything for me. To make my life easier."

His body suddenly lighter, he pressed his advantage. Now his heart raced but for an entirely different reason. It was finally time to tell her everything. A sense of contentment flooded his nerve endings because it could never be wrong to love someone the way he loved Allison.

"What is it going to take for you to realize I'm not a Boy Scout? Maybe I'm a nice guy, and a great neighbor, but I didn't just do this for you. I did it for me. So I could be close to you, so that I might sneak in a kiss or two. Because, you know, I'm a goner for you. I think I've made myself pretty clear."

Her eyes sparkled and her shoulders visibly untensed.

"Oh. Rowan. I wanted to believe it, but I couldn't let myself. It's just too much of what I wanted."

"And you're always afraid that will be taken from you. Well not this time." He pulled her to him, and she didn't resist. "For the first time in my life I feel like I deserve the best and for me, that's you, Allison."

He took a deep breath. "I dropped Perri off and that's it. We said goodbye. For good."

"Really?" She smiled, her voice bubbly as she reached for him, closing the small distance between them.

"You want to know the reason I kept going back with

her? Because I didn't really think I deserved any better. When you and I started spending so much time together, I realized that my feelings for you went a lot deeper than a simple and harmless crush on my pretty neighbor. When Perri showed up, I just wanted to let her down easy without hurting her any more than I already would by telling her the truth. I'm in love with you. It's been you since the moment we kissed. I can't think of anyone else. I don't want anyone else. There could never be anyone else for me. Am I clear enough?"

"They're the words I've wanted to hear but how do you *know*? How do you know you're making the right choice this time?"

"The certainty. I've never had this sense of peace before. There have always been seeds of doubts in the past. The suspicion that the relationship I was in at the time was okay, yeah, but not great. Because maybe someone else would be better. Now, I know. This is it for me. Forever."

She nodded with a small smile and his heart soared with hope because he'd noticed something.

She was wearing the necklace.

He touched and fingered it gently, let the envelope slide off, revealing the interior message. "You're wearing my gift."

"Thank you for this." Her hand went up to the necklace, too, touching his own hand. "It's beautiful and I love it."

"This was my way of showing you I love *you*, Allison. With all my heart."

"Really?" She smiled through watery eyes. "Because I love you, too, Rowan. I fell in love with you this Christmas."

Finally. The words he'd needed to hear from her.

"The best present I've ever had." He brought her hand

to his lips and kissed each finger. "What I want to know is why you couldn't tell me how you feel."

"You know why. I wanted to tell you, but I was afraid. Remember I told you I've been afraid to voice what I want because some part of me thinks the universe will take it away? And I didn't know if our timing was right because you're just off a breakup and—"

"I know exactly what I want. *Who* I want. You're my person. You were right in front of me for the longest time. But I wish I'd seen it sooner."

"Me, too." She threaded her fingers through his hair. "I don't want to waste any more time. When you know, you know. And you're the one for me."

"Can I have the ring?" He held out his hand.

"Y-you want it back?"

Her brow wrinkled and he realized he better hurry this up. "Just for a second."

He didn't want to wait another minute to start the rest of his life, and this had to be done. There were no doubts. Zero hesitation.

She slipped off the ring with shaking fingers and set it in his open palm.

"Here."

The minute the ring was back in his hand, he dropped to one knee.

Allison's hand flew over her mouth. He didn't know if this was a good thing, or a bad one. She was either happy and shocked, or unsure about this next step coming so quickly. He could have planned this better, but the moment felt right. It was his way of assuring her that he was in all the way. He didn't want to marry Perri, but not because he wasn't *ready* to get married. He wanted to marry the woman he loved.

Allison Taylor.

"I love you. Please marry me. I know it's quick. But it was that way for my parents, too, and this is right. I should probably wait until we go back home, date a while, move in together and all that stuff. The usual way. But why wait another second when I already know. I want to marry you, if you'll have me."

"Yes!" She fell to her knees. "A thousand times yes."

He kissed her, a fierce kiss that promised her an entire future of his devotion. She met his kiss, returning it with a passion mirroring his own. Breathless, he broke away and simply studied her beautiful face. He couldn't believe she loved him back. For a moment they simply smiled at each other without words, giddy, and overjoyed.

"Okay." He slipped the ring back on her finger. "*Now* this is all very real."

"No more make-believe."

"I have to admit my brief career as a doctor was incredibly stressful, but I had fun pretending to be engaged." He took her ring finger to his lips and kissed the tip. "Nothing but the engagement itself was actually pretend."

"And, bonus, I already know what a great fiancé you're going to be."

"You haven't seen anything yet." He sent her a slow smile. "I'm going for my personal best. In *every* way."

Her mouth formed an almost perfect circle of surprise. "Do you know what I just realized?"

He hoped her thoughts were going right along with this because he'd also become fully aware of something fairly significant to them both.

Huge.

Life-changing.

"We're alone."

She gave him a wicked smile. "Should we take advantage of this empty household?"

"With no teenagers nearby, listening, hoping perhaps to get tips? I vote a resounding yes."

"I have waited so long to be alone with you." Her fingers glided down his shirt to his abs, eager. "All those times in the past, wanting you, trying not to want you. Now I can show you."

Chapter Twenty-One

Allison Taylor was engaged, and she hadn't even slept with her fiancé.

That seemed like something she should remedy. Immediately.

She wasn't sure when everyone would be back, but she thought they at least had a couple of hours. Billy had given her every indication he would stay the night at the hospital, and the kids wouldn't want to leave until they'd had their turn and seen the baby. With both set of grandparents there, the likelihood was high that the kids also wouldn't come home tonight but instead would go spend the night with one set of them, if not at their mother's.

"We might have the house to ourselves all night. At least we have a few hours," Allison said.

"It's really coming down out there. Seems like people should stay where they are."

"I agree."

She went into his arms, which tightened around her waist and pulled her closer. He lowered his mouth to meet hers in a sensual kiss. It was so good, so perfect, that her body buzzed in anticipation. Rowan made love when he kissed. Hot. Intense. Intimate. She could say with certainty that she'd never been kissed with such passion.

"Let's go upstairs," Allison said, tugging on his hand. "Hurry."

Her anticipation and rush were heightened by the fact she'd waited so long to be with him. They'd had few opportunities and a couple of interruptions, but finally, it was their time.

When Allison closed the door to her room, Rowan's hard body pressed her up against it. Pinning her there, one strong arm braced on either side of her, he seared her with open-mouthed kisses down the column of her neck all the way to her shoulder. Said shoulder tingled and heat spread along her spine, sliding down to the back of her knees. He could probably kiss her *nose* and set her entire body on fire.

As if to prove it, he branded her shoulder with a hot, searing kiss. "I've fantasized this moment for so long."

"Me, too."

She struggled to unbutton his shirt while he pressed kisses everywhere. Her chin, her lips, her nose, her neck, her shoulders. When he shrugged out of his shirt, she got an eyeful of hard planes and brawny muscles. Her fingertips trailed up his beefy forearms to his biceps, luxuriating in their sinewy strength.

"I can't stop touching you," Allison breathed. "I never want to."

"Then don't."

She didn't want to disobey an order from the sexiest man alive, so she didn't.

His hands slid under her sweater and pulled it off, pure heat shimmering in his eyes as his thumb traced the lace of her red push-up bra, then followed the path with his tongue.

Allison moaned. "Rowan."

He slid her down the long length of his body, and she stayed close, wanting to feel him like a second skin. While

he bent to kiss and lick her neck and made his way to the
tender spot behind her ear, she slowly tugged him toward
her bed. When the back of her knees hit the mattress, she
fell onto it and he followed her, covering her body. A warm
surge of pure desire spiked through her, and she trailed the
pads of her fingers down the long and lean muscles of his
chest to his abs. He groaned with pleasure.

He was so gorgeous, a light smattering of dark hairs on
his brawny chest. Perfect. Speechless for a moment at his
utter male beauty, she let her fingers do the talking. Then,
when she could, she confessed, "I want you so much."

She managed to wriggle out of her jeans with him braced
above her and assisting, smiling as though he was enjoying the show.

He stood to unbutton and slowly remove his slacks. As
he did so, he turned slightly and she got an eyeful of what
she'd pictured for so long in her fantasies. He didn't disappoint. He had strong muscular thighs and an incredible
butt. He was hard all over, too, which became obvious the
moment he was down to his tight boxers, ready to spring
out of them.

Rowan took the lead and reached behind to unsnap her
bra. Her breasts spilled out and he almost-reverently grazed
a thumb over a nipple then drew one gently into his mouth.
He sucked softly and tugged until she moaned, going from
a light touch to something a little harder and wilder. When
he stopped, her nipples were hard pink peaks. He continued
kissing and licking his way to her waist and then her thighs.

He removed a shiny packet from his wallet and ripped
it open with his teeth. She could have come just watching him slip it onto his hard length. Her body vibrated and
thrummed with heat. She didn't think in all her life she'd
ever needed anyone this badly. Rowan was so attuned to

her, he knew her every need. Wasting no time, he braced himself above her and entered her in one long and deep thrust that made her moan deep in her throat. He moved inside her with slow and steady strokes that had waves of pleasure pulsating through her.

They moved together in a rhythm that gave her more pleasure than she'd ever had. She was slick with sweat, both his and hers. Their bodies were sliding against each other, connecting, and strangely this felt even more intimate than what they were doing. She closed her eyes at the onslaught of intense pleasure as another wave built and crested. It was going to happen. She couldn't stop it now, almost as if her body was no longer under her control at all.

"Look at me," Rowan said. "I love you."

She opened her eyes to see him finally lose his tight control. His eyes bore deep into hers, and he began to pump harder and faster as if he, too, couldn't hold back any longer. Couldn't slow down. And she didn't want him to. She was ready for him. Gripping his shoulders, she met him thrust for thrust as he went even deeper. She wanted to prolong the pleasure, to remain joined like this forever, but her climax hit with a fierceness that shocked her. And Rowan followed her.

Both of them out of breath and panting, Rowan rolled onto his back and tucked her in beside him.

"Damn." He kissed her temple. "I knew this would be amazing, but even I'm surprised by how great it was."

"We're amazing together, aren't we?"

"I'm shocked at how good."

"We simply have a lot of catching up to do."

"And we'll have so much fun doing it."

"We have so much to talk about and decide." Allison

went up one elbow. "What are we doing to do when we get back to Seattle?"

"Well, we're engaged, so we should probably move in together."

"My place?" They both spoke at once.

Rowan chuckled. "Babe, anything you want."

"It will be nice to save on our crazy Seattle hyped-up-for-all-those-techy-people rent," she teased.

He was one of those techy people, but she knew he'd take no offense. She was worried about something else, though she was sure that Rowan could handle it given the way he'd handled her family this Christmas.

"You do realize my parents are going to be a little pushy about the wedding."

"How pushy?" He quirked a brow.

"You've met my parents, what do you think?"

"Do *you* want a big wedding? Because I'm okay with that. I only intend to do this once in my life, so if it's one big party, all the better."

"We could always elope."

"If that's what you want."

At one time, Allison would have said yes. Running away to get married was romantic. Impulsive. She could do what she wanted, even get married in a hot-pink dress if that was her choice. But as she'd gotten older, she'd grown to appreciate family more, especially her mother. Imogen would love to plan a big wedding for at least one of her daughters. She'd had one huge wedding planned that had never taken place, Charlotte and Billy's second wedding was a small affair, and Eloise hadn't wanted a big wedding with Dante. It was a small thing Allison could give her for accepting Rowan and paving the way for her father to accept him.

Maybe this wasn't a merger of two powerful Bronco families, but it was a joining of two hearts meant for each other.

"I might want a big wedding," she finally said. "You're going to make such a handsome groom."

She framed his face. "I love you."

"And I love you. Do you think your family is going to be happy about this, or confused?"

"Are you kidding? My mother adores you. I think she was secretly hoping this would happen all along. As usual, mother knows best."

"I'm not so sure she'll be that happy about us. This all happened so fast. I mean… I get it. She'll have questions. Maybe even worries, which makes sense from a parent's perspective."

He shook his head. "Not at all."

"But how do you know?"

"Hold on." Rowan sat up and reached for his phone. "We can take care of this right now."

"What are you doing?"

Rowan had already pressed a button and brought the cell to his ear with a smile. "Hi, Mom. Merry Christmas."

"Rowan!" Allison hissed, bringing the covers up to her neck as if his mother might see her naked through the power of WiFi waves.

"Great, great. Glad to hear it. Yeah, nothing much here. Oh, except I'm getting married." He chuckled. "*Hello?* Are you there? I'm engaged. To Allison."

Rowan pulled the phone from his ear with a wince and Allison heard the loud but clearly happy and excited squeal.

Allison covered her smile. He wasn't lying or exaggerating. His mother really liked her. She'd met her only once, and she'd been a darling sweet woman who had Rowan's eyes. Now, she could so easily picture Mrs. Scott as her mother-in-law. She bet she'd also like a big wedding for her youngest son.

"Yeah, she's right here." Rowan handed Allison the phone and pulled her into his arms. "She wants to talk to you."

Oh boy. Her first conversation as an engaged woman. She hadn't even spoken to her sisters yet. But Rowan's strong embrace, his arms holding her tight, were the only reassurance she needed.

"Hi, Mrs. Scott," Allison said. "Merry Christmas."

"Congratulations, honey! I can't tell you how thrilled I am. Welcome to the Scott family."

"Thank you. I know it happened so fast, and I just want you to know that I—we—know what we're doing. I really love your son. Very much."

"Oh, I know. Sometimes it happens like this. Rowan's father and I were a quick courtship. Two weeks and we were engaged to be married!"

Allison laughed and talked for a few more minutes with Rowan's mother about possible wedding venues—Seattle or Bronco—until she was passed around to the rest of the family. She spoke to Rowan's father, and then his brother, who sounded just like Rowan. His brother's fiancée sounded very sweet and welcoming. What a great family.

Finally, Rowan grabbed the phone. "Okay, great. We have to go. Talk soon."

"You were right." Allison smiled after he hung up, satisfied that his family wouldn't think they were too impetuous. "But you didn't tell me your parents were engaged after only two weeks."

"Honestly, I forgot about that. They were friends first, and they've been in love for decades. Some people are simply lucky in love." He kissed her bare shoulder.

"That will be us, too," she whispered. "I can feel it. We're lucky in love."

"I'm the lucky one." He rolled on top of her, seemingly ready for more of that catching up they had to do.

She circled her arms around his neck, studying his kissable mouth. "When I first asked you to come here it was mostly to cheer you up. And because I couldn't stand the thought of you alone at Christmas."

"Ah, well, even if it was pity that got me here I'm glad you asked."

Allison felt weightless and untethered, her heart forever changed. All her life she'd dreamed of this kind of love and even if it took a while, she'd found him.

"No, not pity. I should have known then my feelings for you were so much deeper than a crush. You're my person and I can't believe you were down the hall all this time."

Then she kissed him, sealing their love with a promise of forever.

Epilogue

Five days after Christmas

"She's so cute," Allison said of her newest baby niece.

Swaddled in layers of pink-and-white blankets, she moved her little mouth in a sleepy suckling motion as she snoozed in her mother's arms. Finally, a name had been chosen after much gnashing of teeth. She'd been named Clara, inspired by *The Nutcracker* ballet. Even Jill was okay with the name, thanking Charlotte and Billy for at least not naming her baby sister something "obvious" like Eve or Holly.

"Want to hold her?" Charlotte said.

"Are you sure?" Since coming home from the hospital a couple of days after Christmas, Charlotte hadn't really let go of her baby.

To be fair, Charlotte was nursing, and Clara didn't seem to want anyone but her mother either. Her little face would get all red and scrunched up right before an ear-splitting wail and she'd only calm down in Charlotte's arms.

"She's sleeping, so she should be fine. Anyway, I don't know when I'm going to see you again after you and Rowan go back to Seattle."

"You don't have to ask me twice. Fill my arms." Allison gently took the baby from Charlotte as she'd been taught.

"Don't worry. She sleeps soundly—"

"Oh, that's lucky," Allison said.

"—during the day," Charlotte finished. "Nights are another story. I need to take advantage of your willing arms while I can."

"We'll be back before you know it for the wedding this summer. Both Mom and Rowan's mother decided Bronco would make the most sense."

"Fast-track wedding," Charlotte chuckled.

"Well, I can't wait to have one of my own," Allison said, holding her baby niece's hand.

These days it was easier to be honest about her feelings and hold nothing back.

Charlotte quirked a brow. "And is Rowan ready to be a father?"

"Almost more than I am. He knows I'll be doing the tough part. But we've both waited so long that we're really ready."

The wedding would happen first, however, and as Allison had expected, it would be a big affair. Her father had accepted the inevitable and had apparently told his friends his daughter was marrying a Seattle "techie tycoon." Whatever. Her mother was beyond excited, already making lists. Rowan was fine having it in Bronco, which he now referred to as his "second home." He kept joking one day they'd have a cabin in Montana for vacations, where he'd eventually learn how to be a cowboy.

The first time he'd said that, she'd laughed and said she loved him just the way he was, even if he didn't own a pair of spurs.

"Where do you think you'll have the wedding?"

"It's looking more and more like a church wedding with a huge reception at the Heights Hotel. That's fine with me."

"That will be so sweet. The same church where Billy and I almost got married. I hope you're ready for the five-tier cake designed by a Parisian pastry chef and the couture gown from Italy."

"I don't mind. Mom is so excited."

Memories of Charlotte's almost-first wedding flooded Allison. She'd been a teenager at the time and, quite frankly, had found the whole thing so romantic. Now she would be the bride and it was all a bit surreal somedays.

"It's nice that you're letting her have this. You know this is probably going to get out of control. She'll easily be inviting a thousand guests to the reception."

"That's okay. On the honeymoon, it will just be the two of us."

"Two weeks in Paris?" Charlotte said.

"Yes and I can't wait."

Once Charlotte and Billy had come home with Clara, Allison moved out of the nursery and she and Rowan booked a room at the Heights Hotel.

A loud ruckus came from the kitchen side entrance as Billy, Rowan and the kids strolled inside.

"You're getting better, Uncle Rowan," Jill said. "I'll give you that." Allison loved that the kids had already started calling him uncle.

"We'll make a cowboy out of you yet," Branson joked.

"How was the ride?" Allison asked when Rowan made his way to the living room and the roaring fire.

He and the kids had gone horseback riding through the trails. Rowan's cheeks were ruddy and windswept, his hair wild and unruly under his black hat. He wore new boots, since he'd trashed the first ones he'd bought in town. When she'd later heard all about what he'd been through on Christmas Day, and how hard he'd tried to get to her, her heart had shimmered with joy. If possible, she'd fallen more in love with him in that moment.

"Nearly all the snow has melted, but it's still freezing," Rowan said, taking a seat by Allison. "I see you're getting today's baby fix."

"You bet."

"My turn." Rowan opened his arms and Allison handed him the baby carefully.

They hadn't seen her for a few days. They'd wanted the Abernathy family to settle into their rightful rooms. Getting their own hotel room had also given her and Rowan the privacy they'd wanted as a new couple and now she was thoroughly enjoying her nights wrapped in Rowan's arms. They planned to go back to Seattle after the New Year and move in together, but in the meantime, they were enjoying their days in Bronco. And their nights.

"By the way, we saw Baby J at the hospital," Charlotte said. "He was there for a regular checkup."

"Who's taking care of him?" Allison asked.

"Dottie Saunders," Billy said. "But she's only fostering him, no plans to adopt."

Charlotte shook her head. "Dotty is getting older, and I don't think she has the bandwidth to adopt Baby J. Poor little baby boy."

"What about the mother?" Allison said. "Any luck in finding *her*?"

"None whatsoever," Billy said.

Allison couldn't imagine abandoning the baby she hoped to have one day. Baby J's mother had to have been in a desperate situation to have done so. It sounded awful and heartbreaking.

"You look good holding her," Allison told Rowan as she leaned in and pressed her cheek against his shoulder.

He was going to be such a wonderful father someday soon. She'd already seen it in the way he related to Billy's kids, Merry, and now little Clara. He loved children.

"I can't wait to have our own," Rowan whispered softly.

"Why do you think I'm pushing to have the wedding this summer? I can't wait either. I want to get pregnant and huge."

"I hope the baby is lucky enough to look like you," Rowan said. "Just please do me a favor?"

"Anything."

"Don't give birth on Christmas Day."

Meanwhile, one hundred miles away, a gray-haired elderly woman is served a cup of tea.

"Thank you, Victor."

"You're welcome, darling. I love taking care of my bride."

The woman shook her head. "I can't believe I don't remember our wedding."

"Well, darling, you fell and hit your head and that's why your memories are still so fuzzy."

"So, I've lived in Tenacity all my life?"

"That's right," Victor said.

He picked up the newspaper that had just been delivered.

There was an article on the front page with the headline, Winona Cobbs Still Missing Five Months After Disappearing From Bronco Wedding.

Victor quickly took the paper and threw it in the trash can.

* * * * *

Look for the next installment in the new continuity
Montana Mavericks: The Trail to Tenacity

The Maverick's Resolution
by Brenda Harlen

On sale January 2024
Wherever Harlequin books and ebooks are sold.

And catch up with the previous books,

Redeeming the Maverick
by New York Times *bestselling author Christine Rimmer*

The Maverick Makes the Grade
by USA TODAY *bestselling author Stella Bagwell*

That Maverick of Mine
by Kathy Douglass

The Maverick's Christmas Kiss
by JoAnna Sims

Available now!